# MY FIVE SONS

## A TEXAS FAMILY ENDURES THE CIVIL WAR

Robert J. Gossett

authorHOUSE®

AuthorHouse™
1663 Liberty Drive
Bloomington, IN 47403
www.authorhouse.com
Phone: 1-800-839-8640

Published by AuthorHouse 5/16/2013

ISBN: 978-1-4817-4798-1 (sc)
ISBN: 978-1-4817-4796-7 (hc)
ISBN: 978-1-4817-4797-4 (e)

Library of Congress Control Number: 2013907840

Any people depicted in stock imagery provided by Thinkstock are models,
and such images are being used for illustrative purposes only.
Certain stock imagery © Thinkstock.

This book is printed on acid-free paper.

Because of the dynamic nature of the Internet, any web addresses or links contained
in this book may have changed since publication and may no longer be valid.

The views expressed in this work are solely those of the author and do not necessarily reflect
the views of the publisher, and the publisher hereby disclaims any responsibility for them.

*This book is dedicated to the late Shirley Ranker
who convinced me to resume writing.*

# ACKNOWLEDGMENTS

The author gratefully acknowledges the following people who contributed to this work:

Jennifer Gossett Ayotte for her design of a beautiful cover.

Amy Slanchik for hard work in typing this manuscript.

Sharon Slanchik for overcoming adversity to do editing.

John Slanchik for his invaluable computer assistance.

Dennis Ray for his usual great job of proofreading.

Tih Kobolson for her beautiful art work.

# TABLE OF CONTENTS

# CHAPTER 1

### ❧❧❧

# ANNA'S STORY

*H*ello. *My name is Anna Sweeney. I was born in Dayton, Ohio, but I married Patrick Sweeney and came west with him to Dallas, Texas.*

*He had saved $200, but after we bought a Conestoga wagon, two mules, and provisions for the trip, we had less than $30 when we arrived in Dallas.*

*After we parked the wagon outside of town, Patrick rode a mule into town every morning to look for work. Neither of us had any marketable skills. I only knew how to keep house and sew.*

*Patrick knew how to deal cards. He had learned his card skills from his father, Shawn, a professional gambler. We lived in the wagon three weeks before Patrick found work, cleaning up at the Dallas Palace, a well-known saloon and gambling casino. In his job he worked from 2 a.m. until 10 a.m. and was paid $5 a day for sweeping, mopping, cleaning tables, and even emptying spittoons. He hated the job but did it because we were desperate for money, and I was pregnant with our first child.*

*The money he made was barely enough to provide for us and to buy feed for the mules. So, despite my early stage of pregnancy, I was finally* able to land a job as seamstress at Patsy's Boutique. It was a shop catering to the rich ladies of Dallas and their husbands who bought expensive gifts for them. Patsy Weston, the owner, was known to be discreet, so the men customers could also buy gifts for their mistresses without fear of being discovered. Patsy and I became close friends. She liked my work and envied my pregnancy; she and her husband had been trying to have children ever since their marriage five years ago.

Things were looking up for us in the Sweeney family. One of the dealers was killed by a drunken gambler, and J.B. Rich, the chairman of the board, and manager of the Dallas Palace, offered the job to Patrick on a trial basis for 30 days. Under the provisions of the job, the casino would stake Patrick to the poker games and take ten percent of his winnings but would not pay for any of his losses.

Patrick's prowess with cards and his honesty was paying off. Customers told others and word spread about him. Some customers came from out of town to play at his table.

After 30 days, Patrick was summoned to Rich's office and offered the job on a permanent basis. Rich also asked if we were still living in the wagon. After Patrick told him we were, Rich offered him another business proposition. It seems the casino now owned a five-bedroom house they won from a rich gambler, and they needed a manager to care for it. Rich offered to let us live in an apartment over the carriage house in back if we would care for the house. Patrick quickly agreed, and it was in that carriage house apartment that Patrick Jr. was born. He was delivered by a midwife, Mrs. Gonzalez, who was provided by Patsy.

For the next two weeks, I stayed home with the new baby.

Patrick now worked from 8 p.m. until 2 a.m. He would come home, get a nap, and then help me with the baby and the housework.

*Every Sunday morning, we would attend mass at Holy Trinity Church and make a small donation when the plate was passed. It was at this church that Patrick Jr. was baptized by Father Joe Lynch.*

*Every Sunday when we brought the baby to church, he was admired by the ladies in the congregation. He was especially enjoyed by the Mexican women of the parish. Mexicans made up a large percentage of Holy Trinity's parish.*

*After two weeks, I started taking the baby to work with me. Patsy had provided a crib for him alongside my work station. I only stopped working long enough to nurse him when he got hungry.*

*One day when Patrick came home, he showed me the new horse and buggy he had traded one of the mules for. He would continue to ride the other mule to work, and I could drive myself and the baby to work in the buggy. Life was sweet for us. We now had money in the bank and were saving for a house we could buy.*

*Over the next six years, I gave birth to four more babies—all boys, though I hoped for at least one girl. Mrs. Gonzales delivered all of them. We continued to live in the carriage house, but the two bedrooms were getting very crowded. We still had not saved enough money to buy the house we needed, so we made do. We gave up our bedroom to the boys and moved our bed into the living room.*

*When friends came to see the new baby, Patrick took great delight in expounding his theory on how the sex of a child is determined. He proudly announced that the sex is influenced by the sex of the parent who is most passionate at time of conception. I knew this was hogwash because I had been very passionate whenever a child was conceived. Instead of telling this to guests, I just told them that Patrick must have kissed the blarney stone.*

*It was quite a job trying to raise five boys that close together. To* help, we hired Mrs. Gonzales to come three days a week to help care for the boys and help with the laundry. Patrick would also help as much as possible when he came home from work. Baby Patrick was now eight years old and tried to help, too.

Regardless of the hard work, we were a happy family.

Samuel, born second, now was almost seven. Shawn, third born, now was five. Joseph, fourth born, now was three. Mark, born next, now was two, and as the baby of the family was doted on by his parents and older brothers.

Patrick and I were indeed proud parents, especially on Sundays, when we paraded the children into church, the two youngest in our arms and the three older boys helping each other.

Every night, Patrick and I got on our knees and thanked God for our healthy kids and good fortune, even though I had been forced to quit my job at Patsy's. Patrick's gambling had been profitable, and we felt we soon would have enough money saved to buy a small house.

# CHAPTER 2

## DISASTER STRIKES

It was Friday morning when Anna woke up at five a.m. and reached over to feel Patrick in bed beside her as he always was when he got home about three a.m. He was not there. She lay there for a few minutes imagining where he might be. *Did he get drunk and go off on a two-day binge, as he did once before? Did he grow tired of me and the kids and go off and leave us?*

Then she got up and started tending to the boys. The three youngest ones were still sleeping, but Patrick and Samuel were awake saying they were hungry.

She told them, "You boys are always hungry. I swear you are going to eat us out of house and home."

She made breakfast for both of them. After they ate she helped them get dressed, and they helped her feed Shawn, Joseph, and Mark, who were now awake.

As she looked out the window, she saw two men approaching the carriage house. As they neared she saw it was Father Lynch and J.B. Rich.

She thought, *Now that's an odd pair. Mr. Rich is Jewish, so what is he doing with a Catholic priest?*

She answered their knock on the door, and in came Rich and Lynch.

Father Lynch spoke first, "Mrs. Sweeny, may we speak to you without the children?"

"Of course you may, but is something wrong?" She shooed the boys from the room, Patrick and Samuel looking after the three younger ones.

Rich spoke next, "Mrs. Sweeny, I think you should take a seat. I'm afraid we have some bad news for you."

"Oh my Lord, is Patrick OK?"

"I'm afraid not. He was shot and killed by a drunk last night," Rich told her.

Father Lynch told her, "My dear, I am so sorry, terribly sorry."

"What in the world am I going to do now?" she asked them.

"We'll just have to trust in God, knowing He will look after you and the boys," Father Lynch said.

"Yes, and the casino will help too. We had an emergency meeting of the board directors this morning, and we feel our security was not good enough to protect your husband properly," Rich said.

"What does that mean?" she asked.

"Well, we propose to deed over the house to you and financially help you to furnish it as a boarding house. This way you could still raise the boys without having to leave them to go to work outside the home. Will that be acceptable to you?" Rich proposed.

Anna felt as if she might faint, but didn't, and said confusedly, "I don't know. I just don't know. We will have to talk about it later."

"That will be fine. We can talk later," Rich told her.

Father Lynch asked, "Would you like me to stay and pray with you?"

"Not now," she answered.

"I understand. I will ask some of the church ladies to come and see you this afternoon," the priest told her.

Anna was disoriented, sad, and still crying. She just wanted to be alone and try to think of what she was going to tell her five boys.

When she felt better, she told the two older boys a bad man had killed their daddy and they would have to help her with their younger brothers.

Though both boys were sobbing, they both hugged their mother and told her they would help her, and that everything would be OK.

The ladies from the church were very helpful and quickly became close friends of the family.

With the advice and financial help from Rich, the large house was soon transformed into a seven- bedroom boarding house. As Rich suggested, two bedrooms were left as large rooms, reserved for high rollers at the casino. The smaller rooms would rent for $1.00 per night, but Anna would charge $2.00 for the larger ones. One of the large rooms was decorated with oil derrick pictures, while the other one would be decorated with pictures of cowboys and cattle.

Rich explained that most of the rich gamblers were either oil men or ranchers.

Father Lynch had taken control of the funeral and burial, sparing Anna this further distraction.

Anna attended the funeral escorted by J.B. Rich. She did not take the boys, feeling it would further traumatize them.

When the funeral and burial were over, Anna was deluged with offers of help from the church ladies and some of the men of the parish. She felt as if she belonged to a family, the family of the Holy Trinity Church.

For the next ten years, the Sweeney family thrived. Anna hired Mrs. Gonzales as a full-time surrogate mother and housekeeper. She only accepted the job on the condition that Anna would allow her to continue in her job as midwife when needed. Anna quickly accepted her offer.

Thanks to referrals from the Dallas Palace, the boarding house thrived. Word soon got around the circle of high stakes gamblers, and the two upscale rooms were rented almost every night.

Anna hired another widow lady from the neighborhood, a Mrs. Eberts. She was known for her specialty of sauerbraten and potato pancakes. Anna was an excellent cook also, and her specialties were Irish stew and corned beef and cabbage.

Father Lynch had been a big help with the boys. He not only had baptized them all, but handled their confirmations and first communions. The ladies of the church were such a big help that Anna often told them she could not have survived without them.

Pat Jr., now 15, and Samuel, now 13, tended to the horses. They kept them fed, watered, and brushed their manes and tails. They were usually given a ten-cent tip, but one gambler once gave Patrick a $10 gold piece when he saw the care his horse had been given.

So grateful to God, the church family, the casino workers, and the neighbors, every Christmas Eve Anna threw a huge Christmas party, open to everyone who wanted to attend.

J. B Rich always attended, calling it his Hanukah party.

Usually by 10:30 the party would break up, and many of the participants would go to midnight mass. Under the large Christmas tree in the hallway, Anna would often find gifts. Some were for the boys, but sometimes people would leave gifts for her: money, jewelry, or fancy perfume.

She often cried when everyone had gone because she still missed Patrick and wished he was still with her.

Anna did not realize she was saying it, but she had delivered a favorite phrase. Whether it was from a surprise, a disappointment, or as a term of disgust, she would say, "Lord, have mercy." Some of her friends teased her for saying it so often.

None of the boys were ever able to attend school because the chores around the boarding house left little time for that. They did have some home schooling from the church ladies though, and both of the two older boys could read, write, and do ciphers.

One of the infrequent guests at the boarding house was a man named Charles Goodnight. He was an impressive looking man—tall and dark and sporting black chin whiskers and a mustache. He had a full head of black hair, a muscular build, and always wore a clean western suit and freshly shined cowboy boots. Every time he checked out he always complimented Anna on the way his horse had been tended to by Patrick. Seldom did he stay in one of the expensive rooms; instead he preferred the simplicity of the smaller rooms.

One time after he had finished his stay and retrieved his horse from the carriage house, Patrick ran to his mother excitedly saying, "Mama, mama, Mr. Goodnight invited me to go along as a horse wrangler on his next cattle drive to California!"

"Absolutely not. That is too dangerous. I lost one Patrick, and I sure don't want to lose another one," Anna said empathetically.

"Please, Mama, oh please! It won't start until next spring and I will be 16 by then," Patrick pleaded.

"No. Forget it. No. No. No. And that is final. I don't want to hear any more about it," she told him.

To a teenager, "no" means "maybe." And Patrick continued, "Mama just think about it. Mr. Goodnight said he would talk to you the next time he comes. Please, just talk to him about it."

"OK. If it will make you feel any better, I will talk to him, but the answer will still be no," she told him.

During the next month before Goodnight's next visit, all Anna heard from Patrick was, "I want to be a wrangler on a cattle drive."

She decided to do a little checking on Mr. Goodnight. After doing the grocery shopping one day, she went to the Dallas Palace to talk to J.B. Rich and ask about Mr. Goodnight. She told him of her predicament with Patrick and asked his advice.

He told her, "Well, I know he is a good customer of the Palace. I think he is a good man. I know he owns a large cattle ranch up in the panhandle. He never drinks too much while he is here, and he gambles very little. I think he comes here for the food in our dining room. He always orders a T-bone steak with a baked potato and a green salad. He has one or two bourbons before dinner and several cups of coffee after he eats. He is a favorite of the dealers because he never complains if he loses or brags when he wins. Also win or lose, he always gives the dealers a large tip."

"Do you think I should trust him to protect Patrick on a cattle drive to California?"

"Sure. I think Patrick is a man now, and I can think of a lot of men who would not be as good to him as Charles would be," Rich told her.

"Thank you, Mr. Rich. I guess I will at least talk to him when he comes for his next visit," Anna told him.

When Goodnight arrived several weeks later, he and Anna sat down together in the kitchen.

Anna began, "Mr. Goodnight...."

He interrupted, "Please call me Charles."

"OK. Charles, do you think my son will be safe with you?"

"I'm sure he will. I won't be the only one looking after him. Every man on the drive will see to him, as we oversee every greenhorn on their first drive," he told her.

"Please tell me about the drive."

"Sure. We leave from my ranch, head toward El Paso, then west to California through New Mexico, Arizona, and Nevada. We go into California at San Diego, then turn the herd north to San Francisco," he told her.

"But do the Indians ever attack you?" Anna wondered.

"No, ma'am. They know we are just passing through and mean them no harm. They only attack settlers who build houses and barns and plan on stealing their land," he explained.

"You mean you never have trouble with the Indians?" Anna asked.

"Once in a while we run into a small band of renegades who

give us trouble, wanting to be paid for crossing their land. My foreman at the ranch and ramrod on the drive is Cactus Jack. His mother was a Mexican and his daddy was a Comanche. He speaks Spanish, English, Comanche, and Apache. When we run into those fellows, Cactus Jack deals with them and is usually able to give them a horse or two to let us cross their land," Goodnight explained.

"But tell me, Charles, why do you take the cattle to California to sell? Can't you sell them in Dallas or Houston?" Anna continued.

"Sure we could, but a cow we sell here for $10, we can get $100 or $150 for in California," he explained.

"Now tell me why you want Patrick to go with you."

"Well, Anna, he is a natural-born horse wrangler. I have watched him work with horses. He understands them, knows how to care for them, and makes the horses understand him," Goodnight said.

"Would he make much money doing this?" Anna asked.

Goodnight answered, "Ordinarily we pay greenhorns 50 cents a day, but with Patrick's way with horses, I can pay him $1 a day. Also if we have a successful sale in California, I usually pay a $50 bonus to all of the hands."

"Will he be a cowboy?" she asked.

"No, indeed not. He will be a horse wrangler, assisting Jose Torres with the *remuda*. That is what we call the herd of fresh horses we take along with the herd. The cowboys often change horses once or twice a day during the drive. We don't want them on tired horses because they might stumble and hurt the rider. For every drover we take along a string of two or three horses," Goodnight explained.

"OK, then, I guess you have my permission for him to go. What all will he need to take along?" she asked.

"You made a wise decision. We will look after him. He will need one or two changes of clothes, a cowboy hat and boots, a slicker, and a pistol belt and pistol. He will also need to know how to use the pistol," he replied.

"When should he go to your ranch?" she asked.

"We will be leaving the first of May, so get him there by the middle of April. Does he have a horse to ride out there?"

"Well, we have a spare mule he could ride out there. Would that do?"

"Sure. I can fix him up with a horse when he gets there, and he can use the mule to get home when he comes back."

Anna and Goodnight shook hands, and Anna kissed him on the cheek when he left telling him, "Please look after my boy, Charles."

"I will, for sure, and I'll take your boy and bring you home a man," he reassured her.

Anna was 40 years of age and still kept her youthful figure. She also had retained her Irish youthful features. Her red hair did contain a few grey streaks, but they were not overly noticeable.

Over the past few years, she had several of the men in town come calling on her as prospective suitors, but she turned all of them down. Now she wished Charles Goodnight had been one of the suitors. She considered him handsome, intelligent, and charming. And best of all, she knew he would never be courting her to obtain a part interest in her profitable rooming house. She suspected most of the other suitors were.

# CHAPTER 3

ంల౩ ౩ిం

# PATRICK'S BIG ADVENTURE BEGINS

P atrick was overjoyed at the good news. He kissed his mother and told her he loved her and would bring her a present from San Francisco.

The next day they spent shopping together. Anna added some money to Patrick's $10 gold piece and they bought the hat, a shirt, a used Remington .44 Russian caliber revolver, and a box of cartridges. The gun shop owner threw in a cartridge belt and holster in the deal. Then they went by the Palace to tell Mr. Rich the news.

"I think you made a wise decision, Anna," he commented. He also volunteered one of the casino guards, Jack Dalton, to teach Patrick how to handle a pistol. A week later and two boxes of cartridges used up, Patrick was proficient with his new pistol.

Mrs. Gonzales made him a Mexican *serape*. It was a sort of fancy blanket with a hole in the center. It could be worn as a coat and yet leave his arms free. Patrick thanked her profusely.

After everyone had eaten, they all left, knowing Patrick would be leaving early the next morning.

Before the sun was up, Patrick and Anna were the only ones awake. Anna made him eggs, bacon, and biscuits with coffee. She also prepared four ham and cheese sandwiches to eat along the way.

After breakfast Patrick said a teary good-bye to his mother, saddled the mule, and left for the panhandle. He intended to ride hard and eat lunch in the saddle so as to arrive at Goodnight's ranch before dark.

He arrived just as the sun was setting and had missed dinner, but that was OK, because he still had two sandwiches. He was greeted warmly by Goodnight and introduced to Cactus Jack, who would get him situated in the bunk house.

Cactus Jack was a scary looking man, dressed in a buckskin shirt and jeans. His colt pistol hung on his right side, and a huge bowie knife was on his left. His western boots were black leather and were almost worn out.

He wore his black hair in a ponytail, tied with a rawhide strip.

He told Patrick, "Charlie told me to take you under my wing, and that's exactly what I intend to do. I'm going to work your ass off, but before we leave here you will know how to handle yourself on the drive."

Patrick noticed over the next few days that Jack was the only one allowed to call the boss "Charlie." Everyone else called him Mr. Goodnight or boss.

During the next two weeks before the drive, Jack kept his word and had Patrick doing a lot of hard work. He cleaned out the barn and hog pen. Only after Jose Torres arrived was Patrick allowed to tend to the horses. Patrick thought he knew a lot about horses, but compared to Jose he knew almost nothing.

Jose showed him how to clean the hooves daily so accumulated dirt and mud would not cause the horse to slip and maybe throw the rider.

He also instructed Patrick how to water the horses correctly. Jose told him, "Don't ever let the horses drink when they are hot and lathered up; they will drink too much and founder."

Jose also instructed him on how they would operate during the drive: "We'll herd the horses close to the cattle, but far enough away so they won't be a distraction for the herd. At night we'll set up a static line by stretching a rope and tie the horses to it."

Patrick listened carefully and absorbed every detail into his memory. He wanted to do a good job for Jose, Jack, and especially Mr. Goodnight. The next week passed quickly and the caravan of eight wagons, 2,000 head of cattle, and a string of 60 horses would accompany the 20 drovers during the drive.

The wagons consisted of one chuck wagon, driven by the cook, a supply wagon, driven by the cook's assistant, five wagons loaded with barrels of water for crossing the desert which lay ahead of them west of El Paso, and one wagon loaded with empty gunnysacks. All of the water wagons and wagon load of gunnysacks were driven by professional drivers called muleskinners. They had been hired especially for the cattle drive.

Patrick wondered about the gunny sacks so he asked Jack about them.

"Well, in the old days when a calf was born during the drive we shot it and left it for the coyotes to eat. Now we put the newborn in a gunny sack, put it in the wagon during the day, then let it loose at night, and the mother will find it and nurse it."

"Is her sense of smell really that strong?" Patrick asked.

"It sure is. Last year on a drive we had a cow who died giving birth, and another cow whose calf died, so we skinned the dead calf, sewed the skin to the motherless calf, and the mother of the dead calf nursed it until it was weaned," Jack explained.

Patrick replied, "Well, I'll be damned."

As the wagons were being lined up for departure the next morning, Patrick asked Jose about the chuck wagon.

Jose explained that Mr. Goodnight had invented it. He bought an old wagon and hired a carpenter to revamp it into a chuck wagon. It had a lot of compartments with locking doors so the cook could store small items without fear of losing them on the trail. It also had a large tailgate the cook used for food preparation.

"By the way, while we are talking about the chuck wagon, let me warn you about how to behave around it. Don't ever tie your horse to it or hobble your horse close to it. The cook will raise hell with you if you cause any dust to blow into his food. Also don't ever eat from the tailgate. Only the cook can use that. We eat sitting down using our laps for a table," Jose warned him.

"Thank you for the advice. I'll remember it," Patrick replied.

# CHAPTER 4

# THE CATTLE DRIVE

A t daybreak the next morning, the caravan of wagons lined up alongside the herd of cattle. The string of horses followed close behind the wagons. The drovers kept the cattle moving while the wranglers herded the horses near to the herd but separated from them. On the trail the cook only prepared two meals a day, breakfast and supper. The experienced cowhands usually stuffed a few biscuits into their pockets so they could eat them at midday while in their saddles.

Before they started, Goodnight assembled the drovers, wranglers, and drivers and told them, "During this drive there will be no alcohol, no fighting, no stealing, and no slacking off. Anyone who doesn't want to abide by these rules can leave now. If I catch you breaking the rules later you will be fired, and you will be forced to leave with no pay and only a horse and one canteen of water. If everyone agrees to these rules, then head 'em up, and move 'em out!"

And the drive started—heading west. During the long drive, Patrick got to know the names, or nicknames, of a lot of the drovers, but never much about them. He met Frank Bone, appropriately called "Bones," because his tall, skinny stature gave the appearance of a skeleton; Billy O'Malley, everyone called "The Shooter" because of his prowess with a rifle or a pistol. Black Harry was a huge black man with a large muscular body and completely bald head. He enjoyed eating and sometimes came back for seconds. Crumby was the cook's helper. He was a tall, gangly boy of 16 or 17, and was often picked on by the hands.

Shane was the only man that Patrick did not get to know at all. He was a short man, barely five feet tall, and had blonde hair. He was a loner, usually ate alone, and spoke very little. Rumor had it he was a gunfighter and hired killer. It was said Goodnight was aware of the rumor, but was not going to fire any man because of rumors about him.

The first day they were able to travel about 20 miles. They made good time because the cattle were rested, and the hands were not yet over tired from work. By nightfall, Patrick was bone tired. The job of herding horses was harder than he anticipated. After a dinner of beans seasoned with bacon, biscuits, and coffee, he was full and getting sleepy. After he had helped Jose secure all of the horses to a static line, he spread his bedroll and was soon asleep.

Day after day the routine was the same and relatively uneventful. When they were only a few miles from Ft. Stockton, Goodnight galloped ahead to check in with the troopers at the Fort about Indian activity in the area. He returned to tell everyone there were no serious threats ahead, but there had been isolated reports of renegade Comanches raiding farms and stealing horses. This good news was well received by the experienced drovers who had lived through hostile Indian attacks in the past. After several more days, they were nearing El Paso, where Cookie and Crumby would go into town to replenish supplies. They were probably only five miles out of town when they spied a group of ten or twelve Comanches blocking the progress of the herd. Not willing to take chances, Goodnight ordered the rifles to be distributed to the men from the supply wagon.

Then he and Apache Jack, right hands hoisted above their heads as a sign of peace, rode out to talk to the Comanches. As they neared the Comanches, their leader also raised his right hand above his head. Goodnight spoke to the leader through Cactus Jack, his interpreter.

The Indians demanded three horses as payment for passage through their land. Goodnight told them they were *loco*. Their land was further to the south. He then offered them one horse and one cow. The bickering went on for some time, but ended by Goodnight giving them two horses. The Comanches rode off with their prize of two horses.

Darkness was fast approaching, so after Cookie prepared

dinner, he rode into El Paso and bought supplies. That night the night guards (called night hawks) were doubled in case the Comanches came back for more horses.

The following night when they made camp, they were in New Mexico. Goodnight assembled all of the drovers, wranglers and drivers, and told them, "Men, from here on we are on the most dangerous part of the drive. From here to California we will have over 700 miles of desert with danger facing us from the north and south. On the north we might face Apaches, and on the south look out for Mexican *banditos*. The Apaches will only be after the horses, while the *banditos* will be after the horses, the cattle, wagons, or anything else they can take across the border and sell. So look out for Apaches in the day time, and the *banditos* will hit at night. You drovers are to double up on the night hawks every night and you two wranglers, take turns sleeping so you can watch the horses. And most of all, look out for yourself and each other. Now, good luck to all of us."

With the supplies replenished and the water barrels topped off, the caravan headed due west. Patrick got very hot and dry during the hot sun of the day, but at night, the desert became very cold, and his blanket felt good when he pulled it up over himself. Jose and Patrick slept in four-hour shifts so one of them would be awake to guard the string of horses.

The next two weeks were relatively uneventful, except for the day that Bones passed out from the heat and fell off of his horse. He was quickly rescued by two other drovers and rode in the supply wagon the rest of the day. At the end of two weeks, the drive was stalled for almost an hour. A large band of Apaches passed their trail a quarter mile ahead. They were coming from Mexico and heading north. Jose explained to Patrick that the

Apaches were returning from a raid into Mexico. The Apaches hated Mexicans and killed them whenever they had a chance. The Mexicans retaliated by raiding Apache camps and carrying off men, women, and children. The children would be raised as Mexicans, the women forced into prostitution, and the men were forced to do slave labor in silver mines.

Patrick commented, "No wonder the Apaches hate Mexicans."

# CHAPTER 5

୬ଡ୍ଡ ୬ଡ଼ଡ

# FIGHTING OFF MEXICAN *BANDITOS*

They were only about two days from the California state line when a group of Mexican bandits rode towards them, cursing in Spanish and shooting at whatever threat presented itself. The drovers instantly returned fire and Patrick overheard The Shooter and Shane betting on who could kill the most of them. He didn't know who won the bet, but enough bandits were shot from their horses that the rest of them turned and rode back for Mexico.

*Damn, I wish I could shoot like that,* Patrick thought. He had shot his pistol but wasn't sure he hit anyone. Out of the 14 attackers, Patrick counted nine bodies on the ground. Goodnight walked among them and finished off the ones who were only wounded.

Someone asked Cactus Jack if they should start digging graves for them.

Jack's reply was, "Oh, hell no. Let the buzzards eat them. They don't need to contaminate God's good earth."

Patrick overheard The Shooter and Shane arguing.

Shane said, "I won. I got four of them."

The Shooter replied, "Like hell you won. I only counted three you got, and I got five."

Then not wanting to cause an argument that might get both of them sent packing by Goodnight, Shane relented.

"Ok—we'll call it a tie. Sound good?"

"Fine with me," The Shooter agreed.

One of the drovers was wounded in the leg, the bullet passing through his leg into his horse, killing him.

Cookie patched up the drover until he got to see a doctor in San Diego.

In two days they were in the relative safety of California and headed the herd north toward San Francisco. They still had over 500 miles to go, and with any luck they would be in San Francisco in six or seven weeks.

They bedded down the herd for the night. Cookie and Crumby began cooking dinner while Goodnight and Cactus Jack took the wounded drover into San Diego to see a doctor.

With the wounded drover patched up by a doctor, the provisions replenished, and the water barrels topped off, they set out for San Francisco. Once they arrived, they could sell the herd, rest for a few days, and begin the long trek home. Patrick would be glad to see his mother and brothers.

As the herd was moving along the trail, Goodnight was amazed by the constant stream of people passing the herd. Some were in wagons, some in buggies, and others on horseback, all headed for someplace up north.

One night as they made camp, a lone rider stopped by and asked if he could camp with them for the night.

Goodnight told him, "Of course, you are welcome to camp here tonight and even share our food and coffee, but tell me where the hell everyone is going. People have been passing us for a week now, all headed north."

"You mean you haven't heard?" the rider asked.

"We haven't had any news for almost a year. We are driving this herd from West Texas to San Francisco," Goodnight said.

"Well, they have discovered gold at Sutter's Mill, not far from San Francisco."

"Well, I'll be damned," Goodnight commented.

The word "gold" quickly traveled among the drovers. Goodnight thought, *Gold is like a magnet. It draws people from all over. I hope I can hold this crew together long enough to get to San Francisco.*

With an increased pace they drove the herd harder, faster, and longer every day and arrived in San Francisco two weeks earlier than expected.

# CHAPTER 6

# SAN FRANCISCO

G oodnight instantly looked up his usual customer for beef, and instead of the $100 to $150 per steer, he was able to negotiate the sale of the entire herd for $250 per steer. He was paid in cash and put half into his money belt and half in his pocket. Goodnight checked into a hotel and used his room as an office to pay off the drovers, drivers, wranglers, and cooks. He gave each of them a bonus of $50. When it was Patrick's turn, Goodnight handed him $400. Patrick had never even seen that much money before. He thanked Goodnight and put the money in his boot.

After all of the hands were paid off, most of them headed for the nearest saloon. Patrick, Cactus Jack, and Jose shared a room to conserve their money. Patrick decided to buy some new clothes and leave behind his old outfits that were worn out and dirty. After checking prices, however, he decided to wait until he got back to San Diego where everything was so much cheaper.

Most of the drovers were headed to gold fields. The Shooter and Shane put aside their differences and took a job as gold guards. They would be responsible for safeguarding the shipments of gold dust from the diggings to the assay office in San Francisco.

Goodnight's plan was to take Patrick, Cactus Jack, Jose, Cookie, and Crumby to drive the reduced convoy back to Texas. They were taking only 12 horses, a chuck wagon, one supply wagon, and one water wagon on the return trip. He estimated by traveling light and fast, they would be home in two months. After two days of rest in San Francisco, Goodnight sold the excess equipment, Cookie and Crumby stocked up on supplies, topped off the water barrels, and the caravan hit the trail for Texas.

Cookie drove the chuck wagon, Crumby drove the supply wagon, and Cactus Jack, the water wagon. Goodnight on horseback led the way, and Patrick and Jose wrangled the horses.

They were traveling fast, sometimes traveling 50 miles a day. Ten days later they were only two days out of San Diego and made camp. It was a moonless night, and the horses were tired and hungry. After the horses were tended to and dinner had been eaten, everyone bedded down early. Jose was taking the first watch from ten until two, while Patrick and the others slept. At exactly 2 a.m., Jose woke Patrick for his turn on watch. Patrick was still sleepy, but rolled up his bed roll, slipped on his boots and began the night watch to let Jose sleep.

With a cup of coffee in his hand, he walked along the string of horses in the *remuda* to make sure all of them were securely tied to the static line. It was just before sun up when he spotted a shadowy figure near the end of the *remuda*. Patrick drew his pistol and yelled, "Who's there? Identify yourself."

At that point he was hit from behind and fell unconscious to the ground, but was able to fire one shot at the intruder.

He remembered nothing else until he woke up some time later. He did not know how much later. His first vision was one of a beautiful lady applying cold cloths to his forehead. Her hair was a golden blonde; she had striking features, beautiful brown eyes, and spoke with a touch of a foreign accent Patrick could not recognize.

Patrick asked her in a shaky voice, "Where am I? Am I dead? Are you an angel?"

She answered him, "No, my dear, you are not dead, and I am not an angel. You are in Dr. Adams' office in San Diego. I will go get him and tell him you are awake, and he will talk to you."

Patrick had a splitting headache, and he felt a large bump on top of his head.

In a few minutes Dr. Adams came in to talk to him.

"Son, you had a nasty blow to the top of your head, and you have a mild concussion. I'm glad you are awake and talking. That is a good sign."

"What happened to me?" Patrick asked.

The doctor replied, "I'll let Mr. Goodnight tell you that. He has been sitting up all night worrying about you."

"Who is that beautiful lady who was with me when I woke up?" Patrick asked.

"That is my nurse, Wills C. Vandenbergh, and she is from Holland. Here, I'll write out her name for you."

He then wrote her name and address on a pad and put it in Patrick's shirt pocket.

In a few minutes Goodnight came into the room saying, "Patrick. I am glad you are awake. We were worried about you. Are you OK?"

"I think so, boss, but I have a hell of a headache, and I'm kinda' dizzy. What happened to me?"

"Well, three Mexican *banditos* sneaked into camp. If it hadn't been for your gunshot, they might have killed all of us in our sleep. You killed one of them, I got one, and Jose killed the other one."

Goodnight and Wills C. carried Patrick to the supply wagon and made him a bed. As they were carrying him to the wagon, Patrick was able to see the rest of his nurse. She had an hourglass figure with beautiful, bulging breasts and the prettiest legs he had ever seen.

Doc Adams had cautioned against Patrick trying to ride a horse, so the bed in the supply wagon would be his mount for three or four days. Goodnight told Patrick, "I sure am glad you are OK. I promised your mother I would take care of you, and if you had been hurt, her Irish temper might have made her kill me," and he laughed.

Patrick replied, "Please don't tell her I killed anyone. She might kill me."

"I promise, but I will tell her you are a hero and that you saved all of our lives."

The wagon rejoined the caravan, and after congratulations from the other hands, they made their way to the east.

In less than two months, they were back at Goodnight's ranch.

Unbeknownst to Patrick, Goodnight knew Patrick had not been able to buy presents for his family, so he had done his shopping for him. At the ranch he gave the presents to Patrick.

For his mother, a cameo, carved in Mexico.

For Samuel and Shawn, pocket knives. For Joseph and Mark, carved wooden pistols. After spending the night in the bunkhouse, Patrick had breakfast with his friends, said good-bye to Goodnight and his fellow travelers, mounted his mule, and rode toward Dallas. He would never have admitted it, but he was homesick and would be glad to see his mother and brothers. He was glad to see the boarding house and rushed inside to see his family.

After much hugging and kissing, they gathered at the kitchen table. Patrick apologized to his mother for not writing more often, but she told him to hush. Goodnight had sent her a telegram from San Diego, advising her they were starting home, and telling her she should be proud of Patrick. He was a good wrangler. Patrick was bone-tired, but he did stay awake long enough to eat a sandwich and pass out the presents Goodnight had provided, saying he would tell them all about the trip over breakfast. Patrick went to bed and slept ten hours in his comfortable bed.

The next morning Patrick had breakfast with the family in

the kitchen. His mother was busy feeding the boarders in the dining room. His brothers asked a lot of questions.

"Did you see any Indians?"

"Yes."

"Did you kill any Indians?"

"No."

"Where did you buy our presents?"

"San Diego."

"What were the men like that you worked with?"

"All are different. One Apache Indian, one Mexican, and the rest just plain cowboys, except for one gunfighter named Shane."

"Did you see any gold in California?"

"No. The gold was all up in the hills a good way from San Francisco."

Then the mother returned to the kitchen. She thanked Patrick for the beautiful cameo, saying she always had wanted one. After breakfast the younger boys got busy with their chores, while Patrick and Anna sat and talked over cups of coffee.

"Son, what are your plans now?" Anna asked.

"I really haven't thought about it much. I hear everyone talking about how if Lincoln is elected president next year, a lot of southern states will secede from the union, and that would mean war between the north and the south. If that happens, I would probably have to go into the army," Patrick told her.

"Oh, Patrick, don't talk that way. I don't want you going off again," Anna told him.

"Oh, yes, Mama. I made $400 for the trip, and I want to give you $300 of it and use some of it to buy some new clothes and boots. I have worn these for a year and they are worn out, and I might even buy a horse and saddle," he told her.

"I'll keep the money for you, but I don't really need it. The boarding house is flourishing and I've managed to save quite a bit of money. After you get your new clothes, go see Mr. Rich at the Dallas Palace, and see if he knows of a job you might want to do. I realize you are a man now and don't want to work in your mother's boarding house, but I hope you will still want to live with us," she explained.

"I sure do want to stay here, Mama, but I will pay you rent, just like any other boarder," he said.

Patrick's first stop was at the Clothes Emporium.

He left there with two new pairs of jeans, two new western shirts, and a new pair of boots. He put his old clothes in a bag to take home.

His next stop was at a barber shop, where he got a haircut, shave, and a bath. Then as his mother suggested, he stopped by the Dallas Palace to see Mr. Rich.

"Patrick, how are you? Home from the cattle drive, are you?" Rich greeted him.

"Yes, sir. I am home and looking for a job. Momma thought you might give me an idea of where to look," Patrick responded.

"You still good with horses?" Rich asked.

"Yes, sir. Me and another feller wrangled a big string of horses from west Texas to San Francisco," Patrick answered.

"Well, it just so happens I just bought a stable of thoroughbred race horses, and I need someone to be a trainer and sometime jockey. If you're interested, I can pay you $15 a week, and ten per cent of the winnings, if any. Are you interested?"

"Yes, sir! I would love to do that. Thank you!" Patrick responded, his excitement evident.

"Good enough, then. I'll pick you up at eight Monday morning and show you the horses," Rich told him.

Excited, Patrick went straight home to share the news with his mother and brothers.

# CHAPTER 7

# A New Career for Patrick

For the next two years, Patrick trained Rich's horses and sometimes rode one of them in races. He traveled all over Texas and Oklahoma, entering horses in the racing circuit. He often rode in races, winning some, but losing more. In the meantime, his brother Samuel, who was two years younger, had taken charge of the guest's horses, and was also very skilled in handling horses.

In November of 1860, Abraham Lincoln was elected president and prepared to take office in January 1861.

Knowing Lincoln had promised to make slavery illegal, many of the southern states, including Texas, were talking secession. They knew if they did secede, it would mean war with the northern states, so both sides prepared for war.

During the time spent in the stables Patrick came in contact with many varied characters, some good, some bad. Tony the tout was a sleazy-looking character who wandered around talking to trainers, owners, jockeys, and handlers. He was attempting to find out inside information to publish in his tip sheet, which he sold to track gamblers.

Benny the Bookie was well known for trying to fix races so he could collect large winnings. He once offered Patrick $50 to make sure his horse came in no better than fourth. Patrick refused the bribe and reported Benny to track officials.

The favorite of all the people Patrick met was a recent graduate of the Virginia Military Institute named Dick Dowling. He was only a few years older than Patrick. Dick had been offered a commission of lieutenant in the Union Army but refused it, knowing war was imminent, and his sympathies belonged to the South. Patrick and Dick became good friends. They took many meals together, and spent other free time together talking and sharing future plans and dreams. When it came time to part company, they agreed to keep in touch through letters. They exchanged addresses and went their separate ways.

# CHAPTER 8

# THE SOLDIERS GO TO WAR

W hen Patrick returned home, he heard the talk of war preparations. Texas had joined with the other southern states. The talk upset Anna, and the talk of conscription of all young Texas young men upset her even more. This meant Patrick and Samuel would both have to be in the army.

One night after dinner, there was a family discussion about how they would handle the impending problem facing them. Anna was vehement about one thing: she did not want them serving together in the same unit. Her thinking was if disaster befell one unit she would lose one son, not two. Their discussion lasted on and off for several days.

Then one day a letter arrived from Dick Dowling. This would make the decision for them.

Dick repeated he had been commissioned a lieutenant in the Davis Guard Artillery Regiment and was commanding artillery out of Fort Griffith at Sabine Pass in Jefferson County.

He invited Patrick to join him, saying he would enjoy the regiment because it was made up mostly of Irishmen.

Patrick quickly wrote him back, telling him their mother did not want them serving together so he was sending his younger brother Samuel to serve under Dick, and would appreciate it if Dick would look after him.

Samuel left on horseback for Fort Griffith. It took him four days of hard riding and camping out until he arrived at Fort Griffith and was directed to Sabine Pass to meet Dick Dowling.

After he left, Patrick heard his mother crying in her bedroom. Because he was older, more experienced, and had already been in gunfights, he felt Samuel would need more guidance than he did. After all, he spent a year on the cattle drive had been in gun battles, and even killed a man.

The next morning Patrick went by the armory to check on where he might want to serve the Confederacy. He learned there was a detachment of cavalry leaving in 20 days for West Texas to liberate Fort Stockton from the Union Army. Fort Stockton was located at Comanche Springs, and it upset Texas generals to have a Union fort operating in Texas.

He further learned there would be a place for him in the detachment, but first he would have to complete two weeks of military training at the armory.

# CHAPTER 9

꘎꘎꘎

# PATRICK AND SAMUEL GO TO WAR

P atrick spent the next two days working with his mother and preparing to tell her he was reporting for duty at the armory, and that after two weeks of training he would be leaving for West Texas. Anna was not happy to get the news but happy both of her sons would be serving in Texas, not some far-off battlefield in a place she had never even heard of.

The night before he was to leave, he had a meeting with his younger brothers and told them, "I'm counting on you three to grow up in a hurry and take care of Mama while Samuel and I go off to fight the Yankees. Can you do that for me?"

Shawn, Joseph, and Mark all told him they would do so.

Patrick left after breakfast the next morning after a lot of kissing and hugging. He knew his mother would be crying again tonight, and he was sorry about that but it couldn't be helped. If he didn't join the unit of his choice, he would be conscripted into some unit and who knows where he would end up.

At the armory, he was outfitted with whatever uniform parts they had. There was a severe shortage of uniforms, so they were distributed as best they could. In Patrick's case he was issued a tunic and hat, but there were no trousers available to fit him, so he would be allowed to continue wearing his jeans. There was also a shortage of firearms, so Patrick was allowed to continue to wear his pistol. Normally only officers carried side arms, but this rag-tag bunch was far from a normal army. Patrick was also issued a rifled musket.

Patrick spent the next two weeks learning the ins and outs of army life. He was taught:

Military Courtesy: who to salute, when to salute, etc.

Target Practice: Patrick got used to loading and shooting the rifled musket and got proficient in using it.

Bayonet Fighting: While he could never imagine himself sticking anyone with his bayonet, he did pay attention to lessons and did learn how it was used.

Horseback Training: Patrick learned how to ride in different formations, how to shoot from horseback, and how to care for his mount.

Close-order Drill: Patrick and the others learned how to march, do about faces, right faces, left faces, attention, and parade rest. The group was taught how to form into groups on horseback. They also soon learned bugle calls and how to respond to each one of them.

When their training was completed, the whole unit was broken up into eight-man squads, each under the command of a sergeant.

Patrick was assigned to Sergeant Boone's first squad. Boone was a veteran of four years in the Union Army, but his sympathies belonged to Texas and the Confederate Army. He was a huge man, with oversized hands and feet. His stomach betrayed his love of food and beer. While Patrick knew some of the troops in the other squads, he became close with the seven others in his squad:

John Puskar—nicknamed Pushcart.

Billy Bohn—called Bones.

Shawn McNamara—nicknamed Irish.

Paul Hagan—referred to as Hag Man.

Ben Bohan—called Bohank.

Jerry Jones—nicknamed Jonesy.

And because they knew Patrick had once raced horses, they called him the Jockey. Sergeant Boone's squad was assigned to the second platoon, led by Lieutenant Bob O'Leary.

The second week of August the army, commanded by Colonel Charles Mallory, four platoons of 38 men each, two supply wagons, and two cooks, set out for Comanche Wells in West Texas to hopefully liberate Fort Stockton from the Yankee Army.

Patrick found Sergeant Boone to be fair but strict. On the trail to Fort Stockton, he would assemble his squad around the campfire and give them advice on how to stay alive. He also asked them questions about their backgrounds and experiences. After he had questioned them all extensively, one night he made an announcement, "I have conferred with Lieutenant O'Leary, and because of his experience as a horse wrangler on a cattle drive, and because he is a survivor of a gun battle with Mexican banditos, Patrick is being promoted to corporal. He will be in charge of this squad in my absence."

Patrick's fellow squad members gathered around him and gave him congratulations and pats on the back. Then Boone continued, "Patrick, you go see the supply wagon driver, and tell him I said to dig you out corporal stripes and sew them on your tunic."

"Yes, sir," Patrick said, and left to find the supply wagon driver. After he left, Boone cautioned the other seven members of the squad, saying, "Don't let me hear of any disrespect or disobedience from you troopers, or you'll hear from me."

After a few more camps, a scout returned and announced that they were less than a day's march from Fort Stockton.

Colonel Mallory ordered Lieutenant O'Leary to take a detachment of men and scout out the strength of the enemy at the fort.

O'Leary chose Sergeant Boone and his squad, so shortly after midnight they left so as to travel while it was dark and arrive at Fort Stockton at first light. Boone calculated they would have the sun at their backs, giving them a distinct advantage in the event of a firefight. They saw no sentries on the walls. O'Leary sent Boone and Sweeney to approach the fort's gates and go inside if possible. As they neared, the only sign of life was an encampment of friendly Comanches who camped by the gates of the fort for protection.

Upon questioning the Indians, they learned the last of the ten remaining Yankee soldiers had shed their uniforms and deserted to Mexico in civilian clothes.

The men had mixed emotions about finding the fort deserted. They felt relief there would be no battle, but disappointment they could not kill any enemy soldiers.

After conferring with O'Leary, Boone yelled to Jones, "Jones, you have the fastest horse. Ride like hell back to the regiment and report to Colonel Mallory that the fort is deserted."

"Will do, Sergeant," Jones replied and galloped off.

O'Leary led the balance of the men into the fort. They found that the Yanks had abandoned their heavy weapons. Canons on the walls were still in place, and there was even a stack of Yankee uniforms piled in the corner of the first building they searched.

They found a telegraph key, but the lines had all been cut, probably in several places, to the east and west.

It was mid-afternoon when Colonel Mallory arrived leading the regiment. He instantly ordered a thorough search of the fort.

The advance party was especially glad to see the food arrive; they had not eaten all day, and O'Leary ordered the cook to make sandwiches for all of them. The searchers reported to Colonel Mallory that the fort had been stripped. There was no small arms ammunition, and even the bunks had been stripped of blankets. The storehouse had been completely cleaned out. Also, there were no animals in the stable.

By evening, the rest of the regiment arrived. Colonel Mallory instantly issued orders to the cooks to prepare supper for the troops and to cook enough food for the friendly Comanches outside the gate.

Then he dispatched two teams to check the telegraph lines toward San Antonio and El Paso.

That done, he had one sentry posted on all of the four walls of the fort. The telegraph inspection team returned saying no wonder the telegraph did not work; not only were the wires cut, but several miles of wire had been removed. Then the colonel wrote a report to headquarters telling them they found the fort deserted. He also requested a telegraph team be dispatched to restore service. This done, he sent a dispatch rider to deliver his report to Dallas.

Within three weeks the telegraph lines had been restored, the dependents wagon reached the fort, and the routine was becoming boring.

To fend off the boredom, the non-commissioned officers offered to sponsor a ball and invite the officers as their guests.

The ball was a lot less sophisticated than those held by the Union Army in days past. Only a very few of the officers or NCOs owned dress uniforms, but no one seemed to object to the uniforms worn by any of them that night.

Along one wall was a table holding two makeshift punch bowls, one spiked with whiskey and one unspiked. The spiked bowl emptied a lot faster than the other one.

Patrick sat on a bench with several other young men, both officers and NCOs. Directly opposite them was a bench full of young girls, newly arrived dependents of the officers and NCOs.

Patrick's eyes were immediately drawn to a beautiful girl, sitting amid the other young ladies. He studied her as she accompanied another girl as they went to fill their cups from the unspiked punch bowl. She had well-groomed blonde hair, falling on her shoulders and framing a beautiful face. Her hazel eyes were accented by the green evening gown she wore. The sleeveless dress revealed her well-formed arms, muscular in a feminine manner. The low-cut gown also revealed enough cleavage that, with a little imagination, Patrick could conclude her breasts were not really large, but just the perfect size for her athletic build. Her often-used smile revealed a set of perfect white teeth. He wanted to know more about her, and not knowing who to ask, he moved over and took a seat next to Lieutenant O'Leary.

"Excuse me, sir, but have you noticed that beautiful blonde girl seated over there?" he asked.

"Of course I have, and so has every other man in this room," O'Leary answered.

"Then tell me sir, why has no one asked her to dance?" Patrick wondered.

"Well, Patrick, that is Patricia Mallory, the daughter of our commanding officer, Charles Mallory, and everyone is afraid of her daddy," came the answer.

O'Leary lowered his voice and told Patrick, "They call Colonel Mallory Charging Charlie, behind his back. As the story goes, Colonel Mallory was leading a detachment of troopers when they were attacked by a superior force of Apaches. Instead of the usual tactic of seeking shelter, Charlie drew his saber, wheeled his horse around, ordered the bugler to sound charge, and attacked the Apaches. They were so taken aback at his tactic that they scattered, and Charlie's detachment escaped with no injuries at all."

"Wow, that's some story. I can see why everyone is afraid of him," Patrick said. "Thank you, sir. Now I understand, but if you will excuse me, I think I will go ask Miss Mallory to dance," Patrick said.

"Well, it's your funeral," O'Leary cautioned him.

And he left, heading for the string of girls sitting across the room.

"Excuse me, Miss Mallory. I am Corporal Patrick Sweeney and wondered if you would like to dance?"

"I would love to, but please call me Patricia, and I will call you Patrick," Patricia responded, to the surprise of Patrick.

They spoke only very little as they danced, but after the second dance, Patricia told him, "Please go get us a couple cups of punch, and we can sit over there in the corner and talk."

Patrick returned quickly and took a seat across a small table in a far corner of the large room.

As they sipped the punch Patricia told him, "Tell me about yourself, Patrick."

"Yes ma'am. I'd be happy to, if you will tell me about yourself also."

Patrick then related how his father was murdered and that his mother and brothers owned an upscale boarding house in Dallas. He also related his experiences on the cattle drive, and about how he worked as a horse trainer and jockey. Patricia listened intently then replied, "You're Irish aren't you?"

"Yes ma'am."

"My daddy says Irishmen are good fighters. Are they?"

"Yes ma'am. They must be; my brother Samuel is fighting with Lieutenant Dowling's all-Irish regiment at Sabine Pass. So far they have fought off the Yankees twice and kept them from landing troops there," Patrick said proudly.

"My daddy also said Irishmen drink too much."

"I suppose some do. My daddy drank some, but I never saw him drunk, and my mother won't touch a drop of alcohol."

"How about you?" she asked.

"I have taken a drink or two, but I don't especially like the taste of it."

Their intimate chat was rudely interrupted by the arrival of

Colonel Mallory, who asked, "Patricia, introduce me to your young man."

Colonel Mallory was an imposing man, over six feet tall, with broad shoulders, and large hands.

"Daddy, this is Corporal Sweeney. He is in Sergeant Boone's squad."

Patrick was now standing at attention, until the colonel said, "At ease, young man," and he extended his huge hand to Patrick for shaking.

"Nice to know you, Corporal. I guess you have heard the story about me."

"What story, sir?" Patrick asked.

"You know, the reason they call me Charging Charlie, behind my back."

"Yes, sir. I only recently heard that story."

"What do you think of my tactic?" Mallory asked.

Patrick responded, "It must have been a good tactic, sir. It worked."

Mallory's tone turned to sarcasm, "Well, that's just what I wanted to hear. My tactics are approved of by a wet-behind-the-ears corporal who has never been in combat."

Patricia interrupted, "Oh, but daddy, he has been in combat. He was on a cattle drive from Texas to California, and they had to fight Apaches and Mexican banditos."

The colonel asked Patrick, "Is that true, boy?"

"Yes, sir. It is true. I was a wrangler on Mr. Goodnight's cattle drive."

"Ever kill anybody?"

"Yes, sir. I know I killed at least one bandito who was trying to rustle our horses."

The colonel's tone softened, as he said, "Good for you, Corporal. We can use a man like you in the regiment. Now you two kids go right on with your conversation." And he left them alone.

Patricia told Patrick, "Congratulations! I think you passed Daddy's inspection. He has been overly protective of me ever since mother died four years ago."

"Well, I'm glad I passed. I thought he was going to run me off for sure. I was afraid he might object, and I would like to see you again."

"I would like that, too," she responded.

"Maybe when I have a day off we can go riding together," Patrick suggested.

"I would like that very much," she responded.

The small make-shift band was now playing "Goodnight Ladies," so it was time to say goodnight. After they danced the last dance together, Patrick was pleasantly surprised when Patricia kissed him, not on the cheek, but a full, wet, mouth-to-mouth kiss, and she held him close. Patrick felt like he was walking on air as he made his way back to the barracks.

That night Patrick had trouble going to sleep, still feeling that wet kiss Patricia had given him. Finally, still thinking of her, he dozed off.

Revile at six and Patrick arose, dressed, and rushed outside to stand formation. After the roll call and inspection, he joined the other troopers for breakfast in the mess hall. After eating ham, eggs, and biscuits, Patrick went back to his bunk and wrote a letter to Wills C. in San Diego. He had only written her once since his concussion, but he continued to carry her name and address in his shirt pocket since he first met her.

This letter told her of his assignment to Fort Stockton and that he was now a corporal. He also invited her to write to him, and he was sure to include his new address in his letter.

Now with the telegraph service restored, Colonel Mallory advised his superiors in Dallas of the situation at the fort and requested further instructions.

Two days later, an answer arrived telling the colonel to leave two squads behind to guard the fort and return with the rest of his command to Dallas for reassignment.

The announcement was made at the next day's formation, and Patrick thought, *Oh no. I'm going to be stranded out here in this God-forsaken place, and Patricia will be going back to Dallas with the rest of the regiment.*

His fears were unfounded as later it was announced that the third and fourth squad would remain at the fort, and the first and second squad would be returning to Dallas.

# CHAPTER 10

❧ ❧

# BACK TO DALLAS

The trip back to Dallas was uneventful as far as hostile attacks were concerned, but very eventful for Patrick and Patricia. They spent lot of evening times together, and occasionally sneaked off under the cover of darkness and did some smooching. The dependents wagon was sandwiched between the chuck wagon and supply wagon where it was felt it could be best defended in case of attack. A guard was posted at night close to the dependents wagon. But Patrick was never lucky enough to draw this duty.

When the regiment arrived at the armory in Dallas, the enlisted men were all given a three-day pass.

Before Boone dismissed the squad he warned them, "Men, go have some fun for three days, but be damned sure and be back here to stand formation at 0700 hours on the fourth day, or there will be hell to pay. Dismissed."

The men scattered.

Boone spent his three days playing poker, eating, and drinking beer.

On the fourth morning Boone assembled the squad for

formation, and everyone was present or accounted for, except Bones (Billy Bohn). Knowing Bones had always been a dependable soldier, Boone marked him present and went looking for him. He looked up his address on his enlistment papers and rode there. The address was that of a small frame house that barely qualified as not being called a shack.

His knock on the door was answered by Bones. In a very loud voice Boone said, "Bones, where in the hell have you been? I covered for you this morning, but I can't do that forever."

"I'm sorry, Sergeant, but I have a sick wife and baby on my hands, and I was afraid to go off and leave them."

In a corner Boone saw a frail-looking woman holding a small, crying baby. He asked, "Why in the hell didn't you call a doctor?"

"We don't have the money for a doctor," was the reply.

Boone ordered "Get some things together. I'm taking all of you to the armory."

They all obeyed and soon they were all at the armory. After conferring with Lieutenant O'Leary and Colonel Mallory, Boone arranged for them all to be housed in a room in the officers' quarters with the regimental doctor attending them.

After examining them, the doctor announced, "This baby has pneumonia, and this lady is malnourished. The baby would have been dead in 24 hours without treatment."

He had the baby placed in an oxygen tent and ordered a special diet for the mother.

Both Bones and his wife could not thank Boone and the doctor enough.

Then Boone told them, "You stay here until your family is well, then I will arrange to get a hardship discharge, and you can get a job paying more than a private's pay and support your family better."

When the other troops found out what Boone did, they commented that behind that giant hard-boiled body of a man was a man with a heart of gold.

# CHAPTER 11

ও৫ ৯৫

# TRAGEDY STRIKES THE SWEENEY FAMILY AGAIN

Patrick asked Colonel Mallory's permission to take Patricia to meet his family. As it turned out, he was sorry he did, because when they arrived at the boarding house they found the entire family in tears. They had just been informed that Samuel had been killed at Sabine Pass. The cannon he was assigned to was the only cannon hit by Yankee cannon fire, and the entire crew was killed. Seeing the grieving his family was experiencing, he did a quick introduction to his family then left to return Patricia to her father.

When they reached the armory, they saw Colonel Mallory, and Patricia rushed to him to give him the sad news. Mallory told Patrick, "Son, I am sorry for the loss of your brother. You go on home, and I'll tell Sergeant Boone to do the paperwork to give you ten days leave."

"Thank you, sir," Patrick replied.

Then right under her dad's eyes, Patricia gave Patrick a huge kiss on the lips, holding him close.

Patrick sneaked a look at the Colonel, but only a faint smile was on his face, instead of a scowl.

Patrick then returned home to be with his family.

When he arrived he found Father Lynch and J.B. Rich there consoling his mother.

After hugging him, his mother showed him the letter she received from Lieutenant Dowling. It read:

> *Dear Mrs. Sweeney,*
>
> *I am so sorry to have to inform you of the death of your son Samuel. He died bravely in the line of duty while defending Sabine Pass from an attempted invasion by Union Army and naval forces. His entire team of cannoneers was killed instantly when their cannon was hit by an enemy cannon ball. He died a hero defending the Confederacy. He will be given a military hero's funeral along with the entire crew of cannoneers. My condolences to you, Patrick, and your family.*
>
> *Signed,*
> *Richard W. Dowling*
> *Lieutenant Army of the*
> *Confederate States of America*

Patrick was openly sobbing by the time he finished the letter, and Father McGuire hurried to console him. In addition to his mother's tears, his three younger brothers were also crying. As an outpouring of grief, Shawn announced, "I'm going to enlist and kill some Yankees to get even."

No one objected or responded, allowing him to grieve in

his own juvenile way. In a few minutes three of the ladies from church arrived with three large trays of food.

After the traditional Irish wake, the visitors gradually left. With his mother somewhat calmed down, Patrick went to his room. He went to bed and tried to sleep. His body was tired, but his mind was still going a mile a minute. It was almost dawn before his mind also managed to sleep.

The next morning the family all met for breakfast. His mother's eyes were still red and swollen, but she insisted on fixing breakfast for everyone.

After breakfast Shawn saddled his horse and rode off. He said nothing to anyone, just rode away. The family thought nothing of it, thinking he just wanted to grieve by himself.

After breakfast J.B. Rich came by. He had really been a friend to the Sweeney family, and the older boys thought he was sweet on their mother. They were right. Patrick and his brothers went to tend to the guest's horses and to leave Rich alone with their mother.

That evening when the family gathered for supper, Shawn returned. His mother asked, "Shawn, where were you all day?"

"I joined the army," he replied.

Anna was shocked but tried to disguise it as she asked, "Are you going to be with Dick Dowling's cannoneers?"

"I wanted to go there, but the army needs me someplace else. I joined Terry's Texas Rangers Regiment," he said.

Patrick thought, *He just learned his first thing about the army. You don't go where you want to go, but where they want you to go.*

Anna looked at Patrick to see his reaction.

Seeing this, Patrick tried to reassure her by saying, "I've

heard of them. They are a good outfit. I think you will be in good hands with them."

Patrick spent the rest of his leave helping his brothers with the house chores and assisting in the care of the horses. He watched as Shawn rode off to join his unit, then ten days later he returned to Mallory's command.

When he reached the armory, he learned his unit would be sent to the Louisiana border to fight Yankee soldiers who were conducting raids into East Texas. He was delighted to be sent so close to home, but later, after he learned Patricia Mallory would not be going, he was sad. They would be in temporary make-shift camps, and that would be no place for dependents.

One Sunday Patrick and Patricia went horseback riding, and she surprised him with her riding ability.

He complimented her saying, "I didn't know a woman could be as good a rider as you are."

She responded, "What would you expect out of an old horse soldier's daughter?"

Also before his unit left, he was able to take Patricia home to introduce her properly to his family. The last time he tried it was a disaster, with his family just learning of Samuel's death.

This time the visit went much better. Patricia charmed the entire family. She and Anna exchanged hugs and kisses, and Patricia accompanied Anna into the kitchen to prepare lunch. She also hugged Joseph and Mark, which embarrassed them.

Anna told Patrick, "Don't let her get away from you."

After a lengthy visit, Patrick told his family good-bye, as he was leaving the next morning for East Texas. He drove Patricia back to the armory and kissed her good-bye.

She said, "I'll see you off tomorrow morning, but I will miss you."

That evening, Patrick sent a letter to Wills C. at the address he had been carrying since he first met her. He told her of his latest adventures, how he thought of her often and hoped someday to return to San Diego and visit his "angel" in person, but this time not wounded.

# CHAPTER 12

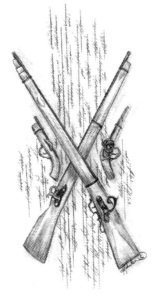

## SHAWN AND PATRICK RIDE OFF TO WAR—IN DIFFERENT DIRECTIONS

Shawn had left three days ago going with his regiment for the Indian Territory to face Union forces at Middle Boggy Depot.

With Colonel Mallory in the lead, Patrick's regiment rode off for East Texas. As Mallory had briefed the unit the previous night, "Some Union general named Banks is moving towards our border, and he intends to invade Texas from Louisiana. We're going over there and kicking his ass all the way back into Louisiana, and further, if we have to."

The troops applauded.

The unit rode hard, pausing only long enough to get a cold lunch and feed the horses, and at night they settled for what the army called "a quick camp." No tents were pitched. The troops slept on a blanket on the ground. They were treated to a hot supper of stew and cornbread. They were moving fast from dawn until dusk, and this time of year the days were long and the nights short. There were a few new faces in the unit, but not in his squad. The new men were:

One-Arm Jack Wilson—Patrick marveled at his abilities to function as well as anyone with two arms. He could mount his horse as quickly as anyone, and if he had to shoot from horseback he would hold the reins in his teeth and draw and fire his pistol.

Spook Sanders looked exactly like a zombie. His face was pale and gaunt, and his eyes were so deeply set in his head he looked scary.

Pretty Boy Johnson was tall, dark, and handsome with black hair and blue eyes. The girls called him cute, but the boys thought of him as a sissy, because he sometimes acted effeminate. Because of this, he was involved in a few fistfights and lost all of them.

Colonel Mallory always rode at the front of the column, the standards bearer on his right carrying the Confederate flag as well as the regimental colors. He constantly sent out scouts ahead at a gallop. They would ride ahead about three miles then return at a full gallop to report to Mallory, then get a fresh mount.

Then two hours later, Mallory would dispatch another scout and the process would be repeated. This routine lasted until dark when they made camp. At night two fires would be built; one large fire would ward off animals and illuminate the camp. The cook would build a smaller fire over which to prepare supper.

After four days of hard riding and short nights, they were entering the piney woods; this area was known for its tall pine trees. This meant they were close to the Louisiana border and in danger of attack from the Union forces headed their way.

That night Mallory ordered the fires built smaller and the guards doubled. The night passed without incident, and at dawn they broke camp and continued riding eastward.

The second scout returned with his report that a large Union detachment was moving towards them.

Mallory quickly designed a battle plan. Half of the unit would take all of the horses and wagons and retreat into the forest half a mile. The remaining forces would stay with him, hide behind pine trees, and ambush the Federals. When the mounted men in the rear heard shooting start, they would gallop forward.

Mallory explained, "Men, if this works we'll chase the bastards all the way back to Baton Rouge. We'll teach them that Texans will not stand for their land to be invaded."

General Banks confidently moved his troops into the woods, completely unaware of the danger he was riding into.

Sergeant Boone's squad, including Patrick, was located closest to the Federals.

The surprised Union troops were slow responding to the rebel fire and the first twelve men toppled from their horses, dead or wounded. The remaining ones either fled on horseback or dismounted and sought shelter to return fire. The mounted rebels rushed in shooting and chasing the still mounted men. All of the soldiers who had dismounted were either killed or wounded.

Mallory counted bodies and saw twenty-two dead and six wounded or captured enemy. His unit had suffered two dead and six wounded. Patrick was one of the wounded, shot in the left shoulder.

Mallory directed the bugler to blow assembly, and in a few minutes Lieutenant O'Leary and the still mounted troops arrived.

O'Leary's men pursued the federals and returned to report they had been chased across the river back into Louisiana.

Then they found Sergeant Boone, who had also received a leg wound. Apparently he had been shot in the leg by a large caliber Sharps rifle because he reported the bullet had shattered his leg and dropped him on the spot.

Mallory, always in charge, barked orders to the men, "Bury the dead Yankees, load our dead and all of the wounded into a wagon, and we'll go to Port Arthur. They have a hospital there, and there is also a Confederate cemetery there where we can give our dead a proper burial."

It was a long trek to Port Arthur but a happy one for the victors. They had run the Yankees out of East Texas, and would do so again if they returned. The Confederate Army had taken over the civilian hospital in town, and the two army doctors worked hand-in-hand with the civilian doctors in tending to the needs of soldiers and civilians. One team of doctors dug the bullet out of Patrick's shoulder, bandaged it, and put his arm in a sling.

Another team of doctors worked feverishly trying to save the leg of Sergeant Boone. The thigh bone had been grazed but not shattered, so the two doctors told O'Leary they thought they could save the leg if infection did not set in.

After the doctors had treated all of his men, Mallory announced, "Thank you, doctors; now you may begin treating the Yankees. They may be Yankees, but they are still Americans."

The doctors were taken aback by Mallory's commanding manner, but they immediately began treating the prisoners.

Then Mallory instructed, "Now let's get these dead men to the cemetery and give them a decent military funeral."

Patrick spoke up, "Excuse me, sir, but I would like to go along with you to the cemetery. I think my brother is buried there."

"Permission granted, Corporal," the Colonel responded.

There were not a lot of graves, so Patrick was able to find Samuel's grave with ease. It was a plain white headboard marked with his name, rank, unit, and dates of birth and death. Patrick made a careful mental note of the grave so he could describe it to his mother later.

The next morning, Mallory left Lieutenant O'Leary in charge of the wounded and prisoners. He instructed them to make their way back to Dallas as best they could. Then he took the troops and set off, retracing their steps back to Dallas.

In the hospital ward the prisoners were not separated from the rebels, so O'Leary ordered Patrick to assist with guarding the prisoners, since his wound was less severe than the others.

That night as he guarded the prisoners, he wrote this letter to his mother:

> *Dear Momma,*
>
> *I am OK, just slightly wounded, so I am recuperating in Port Arthur with other wounded. I should be healed and able to return home in a few weeks.*
>
> *I saw Samuel's grave. It is in a military cemetery here in Port Arthur. He has a headboard, which was properly marked with his name, rank, unit, and dates of birth and death. I feel better about it and hope you do, too.*
>
> Love you,<br>Patrick

The only highlights of his boring time spent in the hospital were the meals they ate in the hospital cafeteria. Most of the restaurants in town had to close because of the federal blockade, but the citizens somehow found enough food to keep the hospital supplied. Sergeant Boone was even able to convince one of the nurses to bring him a bottle of Irish whiskey, which he shared with some of his fellow wounded soldiers.

Sergeant Boone was not healing as fast as Patrick because his wound was so much more severe, and he disobeyed orders by not staying in bed all day long.

One afternoon, a nurse announced there were visitors for Corporal Sweeney and Sergeant Boone.

Patrick almost fainted when Patricia entered the ward with another woman she introduced as Sharon Boone.

"Are you Sergeant Boone's wife?" Patrick naively asked.

"My gracious, no. He is far too ornery to have a wife. I am his baby sister who is following mama's dying wish for me to look after him," she replied.

Patrick looked at her in disbelief. He thought, *She is far too petite and pretty to be Boone's sister. He is tall and fat, she is short and thin. He has the features of a giant, but she is beautiful. He has very large hands and feet, but she has tiny hands and feet. His hair is black and her hair is blonde. His eyes are brown, her eyes are blue. It is hard to believe.*

Nevertheless, she rushed to Boone and gave him a sisterly hug and kiss on the cheek.

Then Patrick asked Patricia, "How in the world did you ever get your daddy to let you come and visit me?"

"I didn't come to visit. Daddy ordered me to stay here in town until you are healed, then bring you home," she said.

"How did you get here?" he wondered aloud.

"We took one stage to Houston, then another one here. We are sharing a room at the Arthur House here, but I intend to spend a lot of time here with you," she responded and kissed him again.

Lieutenant O'Leary entered the room, and announced, "Colonel Mallory sent a wire they were coming, but I was afraid to tell you guys in case something happened at the last minute."

True to her word, Patricia spent all day every day at the hospital with Patrick. Those days he had guard duty over the prisoners, she would spend time with Sharon and Sergeant Boone.

They never got any private time together, but were getting to know each other much better with their long talks together. One day with the weekly dispatches from Dallas, there was a letter from San Diego for Patrick.

Patricia looked at the letter and her jealousy clouded her face as she asked, "What is this, a love letter from another girlfriend of yours?"

To soothe her, he read the letter aloud,

> *Dear Patrick,*
> *It was good to hear from you and know you are safe. A lot has happened here since I last saw you. Dr. Adams and I were married a year ago. I am now pregnant with our first child. If it is a boy we are going to name him Patrick because you were so nice to both of us.*
>
> 

*Wills C.*

Patrick explained, "Remember when I told you about getting a concussion and they took me to a doctor in San Diego?"

Patricia responded, "Sure, I remember that."

Then Patrick continued, "Well, this is the nurse who was the first thing I saw when I woke up, and I thought I was dead and she was an angel."

They all laughed, even Sergeant Boone, even if it did hurt.

In two weeks, Patrick was healed enough to leave the hospital. His bandages were removed, but he still had to keep his arm in a sling.

He and Patricia boarded the stage for Houston. They were the only passengers, so they got to do a lot of hugging, kissing, and even touching on the way. He knew he loved this girl and suspected she loved him, too.

In Houston they had a two-hour wait for the stage to Dallas, so they found a diner and had a leisurely lunch. Patrick had no money because he had not been paid in almost a month, so Patricia paid for the meal. Patrick promised to pay her back.

In Dallas the next morning, Patrick and Patricia first went to see Patrick's family before returning to the armory. Anna carefully hugged and kissed Patrick, seeing his arm in a sling. They also gave Patricia a warm welcome, and they both enjoyed the day before returning to the armory that evening.

Colonel Mallory was glad to have his daughter home, and Patrick was glad to be back with his regiment.

The colonel told him, "Patrick, we don't have a new assignment to go out on, and you are on limited duty anyway, so I want you to spend time here training the new recruits."

"Yes, sir," Patrick responded.

# CHAPTER 13

‧◦❦ ❦◦‧

# SHAWN AND HIS REGIMENT IN INDIAN TERRITORY

Shawn, along with other new recruits and the returning healed-up wounded, were heading for trading post #2—in Indian Territory—to act as replacements for his regiment.

It was only a three-day's ride, but Shawn learned a lot from the returning veterans about the unit he joined.

The regiment was originally organized and led by Benjamin Franklin Terry in 1861. They initially consisted of 1,000 men. The Confederate War Department in Richmond designated the unit the Eighth Texas Calvary, but they were called various names during their travels. These names included: Terry's Regiment, Texas Rangers Regiment, The Charging Regiment, and sometimes as only Texans.

After a long trek from Houston to Woodsonville, Kentucky, they went into their first battle. It was a minor skirmish with Union troops, and casualties were light on both sides, but unfortunately Colonel Terry was killed. Colonel Thomas

Lubbock was selected to succeed him but died of illness before assuming command.

After that they had a series of commanders but regardless of who was commanding, the unit distinguished themselves at Shiloh and Fallen Timbers.

Now the regiment was ordered to the Indian Territory to engage and punish Union Major Charles Willette and his troops.

Willette had surprised a small group of rebel troops at Middle Boggy Depot. Indian Territory, inflicted heavy casualties and forced the rebel troops to flee. The Union troops then marched to the relative safety of Fort Gibson.

After Shawn and the other replacements joined the regiment, they rode straight to Fort Gibson and engaged the Union troops there.

It was mid-morning when the regiment, now under the command of Colonel John F. Phillips, arrived at a point near Fort Gibson. Colonel Phillips ordered a three-pronged attack on the fort. A group of sharp shooters would first shoot the four guards on the log walls of the fort and shoot their replacements when they arrived.

A second group would suspend a large log between two horses and batter down the log gates.

When this was accomplished, a third group was to charge through the now-open gates and shoot anyone who resisted. Shawn would be in this third group.

At noon the attack began. The guards were killed, the gates hammered open, and Colonel Phillips led the charge of his men, three abreast, into the fort.

They charged directly into a volley of rifle and pistol shots, shouting and screaming the rebel yell.

In the initial charge, Shawn was not hit, but he saw the riders on both sides of him fall from their horses, either dead or wounded. The regiment continued the charge, and by 2 p.m. all of the Union soldiers were either dead, wounded, or had surrendered. Colonel Phillips sought out Major Willette and executed him with a single shot to his head.

Phillips was overheard saying aloud, "There now, you bastard. My orders were to punish you. Is that punishment enough?"

The scene of so many dead men repulsed Shawn. He had not seen any other dead people since the body of his daddy at his funeral. He felt as if he might have to throw up, but overcame it. He didn't want to shame himself in front of the others.

A sergeant searched the fort and found a Union doctor and took him to Colonel Phillips. The colonel told the doctor to start treating the wounded soldiers, rebels first, then Union soldiers. The doctor was afraid not to obey.

The colonel then ordered the captured Union soldiers to start digging graves. After the graves were completed, the bodies of troops from both sides were carefully placed in them, and the graves filled.

Colonel Phillips presided at a funeral for all of them.

He said, "Our dear God in heaven, please look down with favor on all of these brave men. They all died defending the ideal they considered to be right and just. Now blue uniforms or grey uniforms do not matter. They were all good, decent, God-fearing Christian men who died fighting for their country. Please protect them. In Jesus name, Amen."

A few of the assembled soldiers had tears in their eyes when the funeral was over.

After the funeral the men found different forms of relaxation. Some slept, some whittled, and others played the harmonica. Shawn chose to join a group of men relating stories of their battle experiences. He listened to their stories.

Mike Cummings had been a member of the Rangers since it was first organized. He marched from Houston to New Orleans, to Kentucky, to Virginia and was there for the bloody battle of Shiloh. There his squad was overrun by the Union forces. He was taken prisoner and sent to the notorious Yankee prison Camp Douglas in Chicago.

"How was life in prison?" someone asked.

"I can't describe how horrible it was. It was near a big lake and the winds off of that lake were terribly cold in the wintertime. The prisoners had no winter clothes and were not issued coats or blankets. A lot of my buddies froze to death at night in the drafty wooden barracks we were in. Several escape attempts were made, but very few were successful. One attempt was initially successful, but the next morning the men were found in a field a short distance from the prison walls. All had frozen to death.

"The Yankee guards were just as miserable as their prisoners, and they took out their frustrations on the prisoners by beating us or just shooting some of us for sport.

"One group of men from my barracks removed loose boards from the floor and after three weeks dug a tunnel under the wall and escaped. They got away, but the rest of us were punished.

"The camp commandant was so pissed off at having an escape on his record that he ordered all of the wooden floors and partitions from our barracks removed. This made our barracks even colder and draftier. Even the dead weren't afforded any dignity. The commandant signed a contract with a local undertaker to make arrangements and give the dead prisoners a decent burial. Unfortunately, the undertaker was corrupt. He buried a lot of the men in mass graves. He even dumped a lot of the bodies into the lake, and some of them washed up on the beaches the following spring. That even upset some of the citizens of Chicago so much that it was rumored they even assisted several groups of prisoners to escape."

"Didn't you have any doctors?" one of the troops asked.

"Oh, yeah, they had some doctors, but they were overwhelmed by the amount of frostbites, diseases, and lack of medicines, and they became frustrated," Cummings continued.

Shawn sat enthralled by Cummings' story. Then he asked, "How did you get away?"

"I was lucky. I was in the last prisoner exchange. General Grant stopped the exchanges when Richmond refused to return black prisoners with the white ones," Cummings explained.

Over the next few days Shawn heard many other stories told by other members of his unit, but none rivaled the one he just heard from Sergeant Cummings.

One of them reported he had been a member of Shannon's Scouts, until he was wounded and returned to rejoin his old unit where he could get medical treatment.

Captain Shannon handpicked two dozen men from the Rangers and former Shannon's Scouts. This unit staged a long series of hit-and-run attacks on Sherman's Army as it ravaged its way through the Carolinas and Georgia.

They would raid Sherman's camps, shoot horses, burn wagons, steal supplies, kill several soldiers, and vanish into the night. On the rare occasion they were followed, they would ambush and kill their pursuers.

These raids were repeated every week, and they created a real problem for Sherman and did slow the process of Sherman's march.

They became such a thorn in the side of General Sherman that he once formed a special force and sent them out to search for the murderers with his angry orders, "Go seek out those bastards, kill them, and bring me back their ears." The searchers had moderate successes, and their findings resulted in over half of them killed by Shannon's Scouts. But that was then and now is now. At Fort Gibson, the 28 prisoners complained violently, as most prisoners do. Lieutenant O'Malley, who was in charge of guarding the prisoners, agreed to listen to their complaints:

#1. The food is not fit for Northern men. We all hate hominy grits, and we have to eat them several times a week.

#2. We are not allowed enough time out of doors to exercise.

#3. The jail is too small to give us enough room to move about.

O'Malley might have been a young officer, but he was a graduate of Virginia Military Institute, a strict school that had trained many no-nonsense graduates now in the Confederate Army.

He promised to respond to each complaint. He started by having Sergeant Cummings address the prisoners. He started by saying:

"So, you poor miserable sons of bitches don't like your treatment here. Well, let me tell you something. I spent a year and a half at your prison, Camp Douglas in Chicago. We were given no coats or blankets, and a lot of southern prisoners froze to death. The food was terrible, the weather intolerable, the medical care inadequate, the guards cruel and inhumane. Conditions were so intolerable even the guards threatened to rebel. Now, tell me how badly we are treating you."

O'Malley then responded:

"As to the food, you will now be served grits every morning for breakfast. Grits, bread, and coffee. That's all you get, and if you don't like it, don't eat it.

"Now to the exercise issue. You will now have close order drill for one hour every morning and one hour in the afternoon.

"About the free space in the lock-up. I am removing half of the bunks so you will have more room to move around. From now on you will have to sleep in shifts, or half of you sleep on the floor.

"I think that covers all of your complaints. Anything else?"

No answer from the prisoners, only silence.

When Shawn and the others heard about O'Malley's response, they all had a good belly laugh.

The Confederate Army was composed of many and varied backgrounds. There were professional soldiers who had served in the Union Army; there were cowboys, rangers, store clerks, bank tellers, law men, and even a few criminals. There was also, in Shawn's regiment, one gunfighter. His name was Lefty Lewis. He was reported to have the fastest draw of any man in Texas. Rumor had it he had killed nine men and wounded none. He

always killed with one shot. He owed his successes to a trick holster. When he pressed his pistol forward the holster opened up, allowing the pistol to be pointed ahead and fired. He didn't have to draw the pistol upwards up and out, just point and shoot. Shawn promised himself he would steer clear of Lefty.

That afternoon, Colonel Phillips assembled the regiment and told them, "Men, I have just received a wire from headquarters. We are to embark on a new assignment. We are being ordered to track down a Creek chief named Opothleyahole and his Unionist Indian Army made up of Creek and Seminole Indians. I can't pronounce his name, so from now on, we'll all just call him 'Chief Oop.'"

This drew a laugh from the troops.

"OK. We will leave three squads here with one of our cooks to protect the fort and guard the prisoners. Lieutenant O'Malley will be in charge. I'll take the rest of you men and leave first thing in the morning for Round Mountain, where Chief Oop is camped."

It was reported Chief Oop had over 1,000 warriors and Colonel Phillips would have about 800 troops, but no one was worried about that disparity. Phillips' unit was equipped with one of the new Hotchkiss Mountain cannons, which could be pulled behind a team of horses, and which was breech- loaded and could be fired several times faster than conventional cannons. It was the first cannon that fired self-contained, breech-loaded ammunition. This cannon would be more than an equalizer and would almost guarantee victory for the unit using it.

For three days they rode toward Round Mountain. They headed up the deep fork of the Canadian River and found the camp, but it was deserted, except for a dozen of Oops' former prisoners who were left behind. One of the prisoners was a young Indian girl. Because she was young, Shawn was ordered to take custody of her and see her to a place of safety.

Another of the prisoners told them Chief Oop and his band were going to another of his camps on the red fork of the Arkansas River. The unit rode off leaving Shawn and the prisoners behind.

Shawn studied the girl for several minutes. He saw a young woman about five feet, six inches tall and weighed probably 115 pounds. She had coal- black hair, worn in braids. She had beautiful brown eyes. Her complexion was more white than brown. And she had a well-developed figure, not fat and short like some Indian women.

He asked her, "Do you speak English?"

He was surprised when she answered, "Yes, I was taught by the Jesuit Priests at the mission where I lived the last four years, since I was separated from the tribe."

"What tribe is this?" he asked.

"I am Cherokee," she answered.

"How did the Creeks capture you?" Shawn wanted to know.

"I was working in the cornfield when they rode up and grabbed me. They are too superstitious to bother the mission, but I was outside, so fair game to them."

"Where is the mission?" he asked.

"It's about twenty miles from here in the direction of that mountain top," she said, pointing to the west.

"Do you have a horse?" he asked.

"No," she replied.

"Then jump up here behind me. I think if we take it easy my horse will carry us double for short stretches," he said.

"What can I call you?" he asked.

"My Cherokee name is Sowohtook."

"What is that in English?"

"It means 'Little Running Bear,' but you can call me Tih, like the priests do," she answered.

"Ok, Tih; let's go," and she leaped onto the back of his horse and put her arms around his chest to hold on.

Shawn could feel her full breasts pressing into his back, and he began to get aroused, but put bad thoughts away for a later time. Right now, he had his orders, and he would obey them.

They stopped at a stream to water and rest the horse. Then they allowed the horse to graze for half an hour and resumed their journey.

By sundown they were beside a large river they would have to ford, so decided to make camp for the night.

Shawn built a fire, removed the bit so the horse could graze, and hobbled it for the night so it wouldn't run off.

Shawn was hungry and was amazed when Tih returned with a catfish she caught by hand. Shawn cleaned the fish and put it on a spit over the fire to cook it. It was delicious. Shawn was using his saddle for a pillow but gave the blanket to Tih, and she slept four feet away.

Before he went to sleep, it was turning cold so Shawn retrieved his poncho from his saddlebag and covered Tih with it. When he awoke at dawn the next morning, Tih was snuggled next to him, and they were both covered with the poncho.

Shawn got up craving a cup of coffee, but that would have to wait. As he was saddling the horse Tih disappeared, but returned in a few minutes with both hands full of berries. Shawn did not know what kind they were, but they were delicious and he quickly ate them and drank from the canteen, offered the canteen to Tih, and thanked her for the berries.

Then they mounted the horse and rode toward the direction Tih said the mission was located. They rode for three hours, rested for half an hour, then rode again, and they were at the mission before dark.

One of the Jesuits saw her coming and ran toward them saying, "Tih, I am so glad you're safe. We have all been praying for you," he told her.

"I was taken from the cornfield by a group of Creeks," she reported.

"Well, our prayers have been answered," he said.

Tih volunteered, "Father, this is Private Shawn Sweeney of the Confederate Army who rescued me."

"Welcome to our mission, young man. I am Father Paul,

and I am glad to meet you. Thank you for bringing our Tih home to us," the priest said.

"Thank you, Father. You are welcome, and I hate to be rude, but neither of us has eaten since yesterday, and I am really in need of a cup of coffee," Shawn blurted out.

"Of course, of course. I am sorry. Please come inside, and I will introduce you to the other priests and get you both some coffee and food," Father Paul told him.

Once inside, Shawn was introduced to the other Jesuits, Father Richard, and Father Bernard. He also met Mrs. Rodriguez, the plump Mexican woman who acted as their cook and housekeeper. Father Paul explained, "We are somewhat self-sufficient here. We plant corn and beans, raise chickens and goats, and sometimes one of the friendly Indians brings us a deer or buffalo they killed."

Tih then interjected, "They also run a school here that is open to anyone who wants to learn."

Father Paul then resumed, "Right now we don't have too many students, but my superiors think that will change in the near future. No matter who wins the war when it is over, they will have to open up this territory for settlers. There is just too much fertile farmland here to allow it to remain unsettled. If it is opened up, people will come."

"I'm sure you're right," Shawn agreed.

"Now, young man, what are your plans?" Father Paul asked him.

"I will be leaving first thing in the morning to try and catch up with my regiment. My orders were to take her to a safe place, and I think I have done that," Shawn replied.

"I understand that. Soldiers must obey orders, but if you

ever need a place to go, you are always welcome here," Father Paul said.

"Thank you, sir. I would like to come back sometime and visit Tih," Shawn said.

Tih had a broad smile on her face. That night Shawn slept on a pallet in the corner of the parlor. He only took off his boots and jeans and covered up with a hand-made quilt Mrs. Rodriguez gave him. He was dead tired and slept soundly. So soundly in fact, he did not know that Tih had crawled into bed with him. He was surprised when he awoke the next morning and found her with her buckskin skirt raised above her waist, and snuggled next to him.

He asked her, "What happened? Did we or didn't we?"

"You'll never know," she giggled.

Embarrassed, he quickly slipped on his jeans and boots and arranged Tih's dress to below her knees.

He and Tih joined the Jesuits for breakfast. Mrs. Rodriguez handed him a bag of sandwiches to take along on his ride back. He told the priests good-bye, and Tih went with him and helped him saddle his horse. As he prepared to ride away, he asked Tih, "Did we or didn't we? I was so tired I really don't remember."

Again she gave him that enigmatic smile and answered, "I'll tell you when you come back to see me." Then she kissed him long and hard.

After three days of hard riding and stopping only long enough to grab a quick nap and graze his horse, he caught up with his regiment. He had only eaten the sandwiches and was hungry for a plate of beans and bacon the cook prepared almost every day.

As he rode into the camp, Sergeant Cummings ran to meet him.

"Welcome back! Did you get the Indian girl to a safe place?" he asked Shawn.

"Sure did. What has been happening with the regiment?" Shawn asked him.

"Well, we keep pursuing that son of a bitch Chief Oop, but he is as slippery as an eel. We heard he was building a fort at the red fork of the Arkansas River. Colonel Phillips ordered a charge on the camp, but Chief Oop and his braves were gone."

"What do we do now?" Shawn asked.

"The Colonel is sending out a small unit of scouts tomorrow morning to try and locate Chief Oop, and if they find them, the rest of us will follow and kill the bastards," Cummings explained.

At dawn the next morning, Shawn watched as the unit of scouts left. He wished he could be going with them.

By 10 a.m. the scout unit was returning in full retreat, chased closely by Chief Oop's far superior force. The rest of the day was spent in a ferocious battle. The Hotchkiss cannon was inflicting heavy casualties on the warriors, and the forward skirmish line also was responsible for a lot of dead Indians.

As darkness fell, the fighting abruptly stopped. The Indians rarely fought at night, as they believed if they were killed at night, the Great Spirit could not find their souls and they would be condemned to eternal darkness.

The Confederate troops were also glad to cease fighting. Some were wounded, and all of them were extremely hungry from having no food since breakfast.

Shawn stood beside Cummings during the battle and the two of them were responsible for sending many of their enemies to their "happy hunting grounds."

The Confederates were fed breakfast before dawn and prepared for a mounted charge at morning light.

At dawn they scouted and found the Unionist Indians gone, having slipped out during the night. Now they pursued the retreating Indians relentlessly and forced them back across the Kansas state line.

That done, Colonel Phillips claimed victory, having fulfilled at least part of his mission: "Drive Chief Oop out of the Indian Territory."

The troops rested the remainder of the day and prepared for the long trip back to Fort Gibson. It took fourteen days, but the troops, exhausted, finally arrived at the fort.

When the troops entered the fort they were met by loud cheers, not for their routing of Chief Oop, but because they received a telegram wire that the war was over. Lee had surrendered to Grant the previous week in Virginia. Hearing this, all of the troops began cheering and celebrating. There were also loud cheers heard coming from the Union troops, still in prison. Colonel Phillips assembled the unit and spoke with them.

"Men, it appears the war is over, and I thank all of you for your service to me and to the Confederacy. OK, we might have lost the war, but now we can all work at winning the peace. Release the prisoners, give them some supplies and their horses, and get them out of the fort. I don't want any of your or their hard feelings causing any fist fights.

"After they are on their way to their homes, we will all

remain as a unit until we get home in Dallas. Thank you all for your service," he told them.

It was an arduous but happy trip back to Dallas for the rebels. They were going home. Home to wives and children, parents, family, and girlfriends.

As they crossed the Red River into Texas, there was a loud cheer. They were really home now. Shawn was happy, but in a way, sad too. He had promised Tih he would see her again, and now he wondered if he could. When they reached the armory, they were anxious to disperse, but Phillips asked for their patience for one more hour. The hour passed quickly with the crew congratulating each other, shaking hands and saying their good-byes to their fellow soldiers.

# CHAPTER 14

◈◈◈

# THE TEXAS RANGERS
# ARE REESTABLISHED

After the hour had passed, Phillips again asked for silence, then told the assembled men, "Men, I have been given a commission by Governor Richard Coke to reestablish the Texas Rangers, a group of law men, under the direct orders of the Governor. We will answer only to him, not legal jurisdiction. We will need 250 men to start, so if any of you are interested, see me after we adjourn here, and I will interview you. I know many of you have spouses and family to return to, but I hope at least 250 of you will join me in this endeavor. Thank you again for your service and God bless each and every one of you."

There was loud applause from the men.

Shawn waited his turn in line, and then asked Colonel Phillips, "Do you need to know today, or can I talk to you about it later?"

"I will be here all week, so come and see me when you are ready," was the reply.

Then Shawn hurried off for home. He was anxious to see his mother and brothers. He also wanted to ask Patrick, secretly, about his encounter with Tih. Did he or didn't he? Shawn was surprised to see the entire family assembled in the parlor when he walked in the front door. His mother and brothers were all there, as was Father Lynch and J.B. Rich. He thought to himself, *This can't all be for me. They couldn't have known I was coming home today.*

His mother rushed to him, almost hugging the breath out of him saying, "Oh Shawn, I am so glad you are home safe. We have all missed you."

Then his three brothers mobbed him, giving him hugs, handshakes, and well-wishes.

Almost overwhelmed, he asked, "What is going on? I thought I would surprise you."

"You did surprise us. But we have a surprise for you too. J.B. and I are going to be married next month," she told him.

Shawn was astonished, but did recover enough to say, "Congratulations to you both. I am happy for you."

Rich answered, "Thank you, and welcome home. Your mother really wanted all of her boys to be with her at the wedding."

Then Father Lynch came to Shawn saying, "I'm glad you are home, and I'm glad you are safe. I think everyone is glad that war is over, even if we did lose the war."

"I came here today to tell J.B. and your mother that I wrote Bishop Sheen and asked for permission to marry them in my church even though J.B. wasn't a Catholic. Unfortunately, he refused but did give me permission to perform the ceremony off of church property."

Anna continued saying, "So J.B. and I decided to be married in the Dallas Palace. There is a private room we can use for the ceremony, then use the main dining room for the reception. It will just be perfect."

"I'm really happy for you two. I know you will be happy together. I also have some news for everyone. I'm thinking about joining the Texas Rangers. My old commander Colonel Phillips is going to be in charge of them, and I have a chance to join up," Shawn announced.

Rich was the first to respond, "I think that's a great idea. I heard Governor Coke was going to reestablish them, and I applaud him for doing it."

Later Anna served them all a delicious dinner of brisket, cole slaw, and fried potatoes she cooked earlier in the day. Everyone was full from the big dinner, but she insisted they all have a slice of the deep-dish apple pie she baked. No one refused her.

After dinner Joseph and Mark cleaned the table and washed and dried the dishes as Anna instructed them to do. Everyone else enjoyed their coffee as they sat in the parlor and talked. Shawn asked his mother, "Have you set a definite date for the wedding?"

"Not yet, just some time next month. We have a lot of arrangements to work out yet. I sure hope you will be here with all of us when the exact date is set," Anna answered.

"I will do my best to be there," Shawn said.

After everyone but family had left, the mother and her four sons sat and talked. Joseph and Mark wanted to know all about Shawn's adventures in the war. He had to choose his answers carefully because his mother was listening intently. He told them, "Well, we all met at trading post number two, then rode over to Fort Gibson in the eastern part of the Indian Territory and captured Fort Gibson. Then most of us went chasing after an Indian chief we called Oop. We trailed him and his band of Union sympathizers all over the Indian Territory. It took us a long time because he was so elusive, but we finally engaged him in a big battle and chased him all the way to Kansas. Then we rode back to Fort Gibson and learned the war was over, so we all came back to Dallas."

The younger boys listened intently, occasionally saying "Wow" or "Gee whiz." Then Anna interrupted, "OK, now it's time for bed. Shawn, you sleep with Patrick, and I'll see you all for breakfast in the morning," and she kissed them all goodnight.

Shawn was glad to share the room with Patrick because he was dying to ask him about Tih. As soon as they were alone he told Patrick of his encounter with Tih and asked him, "What do you think? Did we or didn't we? I honestly don't remember."

Patrick answered, "I doubt if you did. If you did you certainly would remember. Was this your first time?"

Shawn sheepishly answered, "Yes."

"Then believe me, you would remember. I think she was just wanting you to think you did so she could see you again. Women are crafty creatures, and they know how to play mind games with men," Patrick answered.

"I just wish I really could be sure," Shawn continued, not willing to accept Patrick's answer that easily.

"Did you have to kill anyone?" Patrick asked, wanting to change the conversation.

Shawn answered, "Yeah, but don't tell Mama."

"I won't. I didn't tell her either about the men I had to kill," Patrick reassured him.

Shawn slept soundly that night, in a comfortable bed, and thinking he and Tih probably did not do it.

The next morning, before they went for breakfast, they continued talking. Shawn asked Patrick, "I'm probably going to join up for the Texas Rangers today. Want to join up with me?"

"I wish I could, but I promised J.B. I would take over running the boarding house after he and Mama got married. My plan is to ask Patricia Mallory to marry me and help me run this place. She could hire and supervise the cook and cleaning lady, and I could tend to the horses, chop wood, and do the other heavy chores," Patrick told him.

"Wow, does Mama know?" Shawn asked.

"No, and don't you tell her. I haven't told anyone but you. I haven't even asked Patricia yet," Patrick cautioned him.

"OK, I won't. Now let's go eat. I am starved," Shawn said.

After breakfast Patrick rode along with Shawn to the armory, Shawn to join the Texas Rangers, and Patrick to see Patricia.

As they walked through the armory door, they met ex-Colonel Mallory and a Union Army general named Zachary Scott. Mallory introduced Patrick as his daughter's suitor, and Patrick introduced Shawn to both of them.

Mallory told Patrick, "Patricia is in our quarters. Go ahead and see her. General Scott and I have some business to discuss."

"Thank you, sir," Patrick said.

Patrick left to see Patricia, and Shawn hurried to see Colonel

Phillips. He found him addressing a group of would-be rangers, so he took a seat and listened.

"Men, we are about to embark on a history-making journey. We are reestablishing a proud tradition. The Texas Rangers were first established in 1823 and have the reputation of being a no-nonsense peacekeeping group of lawmen. We will enforce the laws of Texas, and the United States, using our brains, and fists, and guns when necessary.

"I will maintain the rank of Colonel, and I will be in Austin, in charge of the special regiment. This regiment will have a special jurisdiction to go anywhere, any time, and be permitted to cross state lines, even other countries' borders to accomplish the mission I assign to them. A second regiment called 'A Frontier Regiment' will be stationed in Garland with 100 men under the command of Captain John (Rip) Ford. I know a lot of you have heard of him. After the war had been over for weeks, the Yankee commander of the Union forces on Brazos Island invaded the Texas mainland and attacked a Confederate fort. Captain Ford heard this news and rode in with his troops and artillery and ran their asses back to Brazos Island and made sure they stayed there.

"A second Frontier Regiment, also with 100 men, will be stationed in San Antonio. This regiment will be under the command of Major Paul (Tall Paul) Evans. He is 6 feet, 9 inches tall, hence the nickname of Tall Paul. I wouldn't recommend you call him that to his face, however. He doesn't like it, and you'll learn to regret calling him that. He has been a peace officer since he was 17 years old and has been a deputy sheriff and a high sheriff. During the war, he led a hand-picked group of men called Rangers. They specialized in raiding Yankee prison camps and freeing the prisoners held there.

"The pay will be $3 a day, and you will furnish your own horse, pistol, rifle, and cartridges. If you volunteer, you can't pick your assignment. I will try and honor as many of your preferences as possible, but I can't guarantee they will all be met.

"I don't have to tell you this will be a daunting assignment. There is always a lot of chaos after a war. We are going to have a lot of carpetbaggers coming down here with carpetbags full of money trying to cheat people out of their property. We are also going to have a lot of young men, ex-soldiers, using their guns to make a living as bounty hunters, bank robbers, and train and stagecoach robbers.

"Now, knowing all of this, if you wish to enlist, see the clerks at the table behind me, and they will sign you up, and I will swear you in and give you your badges.

"I know some of you won't want to wear a badge, thinking it makes you a target. I'll leave that up to you, but remember, it is sometimes easier to arrest someone if you are showing a badge."

Shawn spent the rest of the day standing in line to enlist, getting sworn in, and getting his badge. He wanted to join the Garland Regiment to be closer to home, but he was told to report back to the armory in three days to get his assignment. Shawn then hurried off to show Patrick his badge. He asked directions to Colonel Mallory's quarters and went there.

He found Patrick and Patricia sitting on the sofa talking.

Patricia spotted him first and ran to him saying, "Shawn,

come on in. I was just telling Patrick the exciting news about my daddy."

Shawn was puzzled and asked, "And what might that be?"

"Oh, Daddy has been commissioned a Colonel in the Union Army and is going to lead a regiment to fight Indians in West Texas, New Mexico, Arizona, and Colorado."

Shawn replied, "That's great, if that's what he wants to do, but you won't be able to go out there with him, will you?"

Patrick interrupted, "No, she is going to come and live with us until she and I are married. I asked her daddy for permission, and he agreed, and I asked her to marry me, and she agreed. So now it is all settled."

Shawn told them, "Congratulations to both of you! I know you will be happy together."

Patricia then spoke up, "What are your plans? I see you are wearing a badge. What is that?"

"Well, as of today I am a new Texas Ranger and will find out my assignment in three days.

"I have asked to be assigned to the Garland Regiment to be close to home, but it's possible I might be sent to Austin or San Antonio," Shawn related.

"Then I will give my future brother-in-law a kiss of congratulations," Patricia said and kissed Shawn on the lips.

"Careful, Patricia. Brotherly love only goes so far," Patrick joked.

Patricia went to be with her daddy, and Patrick and Shawn rode home, excited to share the news with their mother and brothers.

J.B. Rich was sitting with their mother and brothers when they arrived.

Patrick told his good news first. Then Shawn told of his future plans.

Rich spoke up, "I knew I brought a bottle of champagne with me for some reason, and now I'm glad I did. I'll go open it and toast these two deserving young men."

Anna stood and hugged Patrick and Shawn, saying, "I am so proud of you two—all of us are."

Then Rich returned with the champagne and glasses and poured all of them a glass. Even the two younger boys got a little bit.

Then he said, "Here's a toast to these young men who are the future of this great state of Texas."

Then they sat talking, and Rich continued, "So old Colonel Mallory is going to be a Colonel in the Yankee Army."

Patrick answered, "Reckon so. They must have heard the story of why he is called 'Chargin' Charlie.'"

By the time the celebrating was over, Anna had not prepared any supper. No one minded fixing their own sandwiches, so that's what they all ate.

The next two days all four boys pitched in to do the chores as they had done so many times before.

Anna and J.B. went shopping, Anna for a wedding dress, and J.B. for a new suit. Anna confided in J.B., "I'm afraid the boys won't have anything appropriate to wear to the wedding."

"Please don't worry about that. All eyes will be on you, not the boys. I'm sure they will have something nice to put on," J.B. reassured her.

The next two days passed quickly, and Shawn was up early to report to the armory and learn about his assignment. Patrick accompanied him so he could see Patricia. He and Patricia had made plans for lunch. Colonel Mallory spotted Patrick and rushed to him, saying, "Patrick, I was just on my way to see you at your mother's house. I have been assigned to New Mexico and have to be there next week. I have been at wits end trying to figure out what to do with Patricia. When do you two plan to be married?"

"We haven't really set a date. Let's go ask Patricia what she thinks," Patrick told him, not knowing what ulterior motive Mallory had in mind.

Patricia was just as stunned by her dad's announcement as Patrick had been.

"Daddy, I don't have the slightest idea of what I will do, but I'm a big girl now and I will be fine by myself. You go ahead and take the assignment, and I'll be fine," she told him.

"Patrick, will you take the responsibility for her?" Mallory asked.

"Of course I will. She will be fine. She can move in with mother and be safe there," Patrick replied.

"OK then, I'll put her in your custody, but don't you betray that trust, or there will be hell to pay," Mallory told him. Then he stormed out to get his troops ready for the long trek to New Mexico.

After lunch Patrick and Patricia discussed how they were going to handle the predicament Patricia's daddy had put them in. They didn't want to upstage the wedding of Anna and J.B. They also didn't want to cause any scandal that would eventually disgrace Colonel Mallory. They couldn't find a solution, so they decided to go see Father Lynch and ask for his advice.

After they asked him, he told them to let him pray for it, and he would find a solution. He asked them to check back with him the next day, and he would try and have a solution for them.

Then they returned to the armory, and Patricia went to her quarters and Patrick looked for Shawn.

When he found Shawn, there was disappointment all over his face, betraying the bad news he had to tell his brother.

"I didn't get the Garland assignment. I am assigned to the Frontier Regiment in San Antonio," Shawn said.

Patrick tried to reassure him, saying, "Look at it this way: you are still a Ranger, and you will still wear the star in a wheel badge of a Texas Ranger."

"Yes, but I sure hope I won't have to miss Mama's wedding next month. I know she wants all four of us there," Shawn answered.

"Let's go home and tell Mama. I know it will all work out," Patrick suggested.

Anna was not happy about the news but told Shawn, "Please don't worry about it. We'll just put it in God's hands, and He will solve it for us."

Shawn had three days before he left for San Antonio. One day was spent going with his three brothers, secretly with J.B. Rich to buy all of them matching blue blazers for the wedding. Rich swore them to secrecy and told them not to wear them until the wedding, so as to surprise their mother.

That same day Patrick and Patricia went to see Father Lynch to see if he found a solution to the dilemma.

Father Lynch told them, "Ordinarily I dislike intrigue, but sometimes God allows it if it is for a good cause. Subject to approval by both of you, I can marry you secretly. Your mother told me Shawn is moving to San Antonio, so after the ceremony you can go with him and start a new life together there, then return in time to attend your mother's wedding. What do you think?"

They were both elated, and Patrick said, "Thank you, Father! That is such a simple solution. How did you think of it?"

"It took a lot of praying, and God has been good to me by answering so many of my requests," Father Lynch answered.

"When can we get married?" Patrick asked.

"I'll marry you just before Shawn leaves, then you can leave with him and no one will be the wiser," Father Lynch explained.

Later when they were alone, Patrick and Patricia planned how they could pull off the reception.

Patrick said, "I'll tell Shawn, and he can be my best man and help us all, but who will you get to stand up with you?"

"I know I'll get Conchita Diaz. I have known her for a long time. Her daddy is Sergeant Diaz. Daddy says he could be a top soldier if he didn't drink so much. Conchita told me once sometimes he is mean to her when he is drunk. That's probably why she is a little wild, but she will be fine for this job."

The night before Shawn was slated to leave, Patrick explained the deception to him. He shook Patrick's hand, congratulated him, and said he would be happy to help. That evening over dinner Patrick told his mother and brothers he was going to San Antonio with Shawn to get him settled in, then return in time for the wedding. He made no mention of Patricia. The next morning Shawn and Patrick rode off in the buggy. The plan was to meet Patricia and Conchita at the church, have the wedding, then take Conchita home and ride off to San Antonio. Patricia and Conchita were waiting at the church, along with Patricia's luggage.

# CHAPTER 15

## PATRICK AND PATRICIA MARRY

Patricia introduced them both to Conchita, then was surprised when Conchita gave Patrick a kiss on the cheek. Then she grabbed Shawn and kissed him full on the mouth. Shawn could feel her tongue pushing his mouth open and begin exploring his entire mouth.

He thought, *Wow, I have only kissed two girls before, Patricia and Tih, and neither of them kissed me like this. It makes me feel funny.*

Patrick said, "Break it up, you two. We've got a wedding to tend to, and it's not yours, it's ours."

They all entered the church, and Father Lynch was waiting at the altar for them. Patricia introduced Conchita to Father Lynch, hoping she didn't kiss him. She didn't.

Patrick was prepared. He bought a ring, quietly, after Rich took them shopping. Father Lynch had a short ceremony, no customary mass, just the exchanging of vows, a blessing, and the placing of the ring on her finger. Patrick tried to pay him, but Father Lynch refused to take it. Instead he told them, "Be good to each other and to friends and family," then wished them good luck. Shawn drove the buggy, Conchita beside him, and Patrick and Patricia were kissing and hugging in the rear seat.

When they reached the armory, Conchita got out, but not before giving Shawn another tongue exploration kiss. Shawn drove off for Waco, their planned first stop on the road to San Antonio. In Waco, Shawn rented a room in a boarding house, and Patrick and Patricia also rented a room there, but on a separate floor. Shawn had trouble getting to sleep, thinking about the two kisses he had been given from Conchita. Patrick and Patricia also had trouble sleeping, but for a different reason.

The next morning, after breakfast at the boarding house, they set out for San Antonio.

Both men were now wearing their pistol belts again, after secreting them in the buggy during the ceremony. They felt better wearing them because of the high number of robberies on travelers on this main road. Shawn also proudly displayed his Texas Rangers badge on his shirt.

It was almost dark when they reached San Antonio. They did find a small hotel where they rented rooms for the night. The plan was for the newlyweds to take Shawn to the Ranger station the next morning, and then look for a place the three of them could live, at least until the wedding. After that Shawn would be on his own, and Patrick and Patricia would take over management of the rooming house and live in the apartment over the carriage house.

The newlyweds took Shawn to the Ranger station, then bought a newspaper and scanned the rental section. They saw an ad for a small cottage for rent: "Furnished, two bedrooms, complete large kitchen, with lovely parlor and a large porch." They rode to the address listed.

Meanwhile, Shawn walked into the Ranger station and met Major Paul Evans, his new boss. He found "Tall Paul" was the right nickname for Paul Evans. Shawn studied him carefully. He was 6'9" tall, with broad shoulders and a barrel chest. His features were not giant like as some tall people's were, but were probably handsome to the ladies. His huge hand enveloped Shawn's as Shawn introduced himself, "Howdy Shawn, I'm glad to meet you. Welcome to San Antonio. I think you know some of the men you will be working with. One-Arm Jack Wilson is here, along with Lefty Lewis, and Sam Cummings is also here," Evans told him.

"I'm glad; they are all good men," Shawn said.

"If they weren't they wouldn't be here," Evans responded.

"I know they are because I served with them in the war fighting Yankees and Union sympathizing Indians in the Indian Territory," Shawn told him.

"Yes, I heard about that from Colonel Phillips, and I also heard from him that you asked for the Garland Regiment so you could attend your widowed mother's wedding next month," Evans said.

"Yes, sir, I did, but I am a Ranger first and a good son second," Shawn said.

"Son, you've got that wrong. If you are a good son, you will also be a good Ranger. Don't worry; if it is at all possible, I will make sure you get a week off next month to attend the wedding, but I can't pay you for that week," Evans told him.

"Thank you, sir," Shawn replied, less worried than he had been.

"Now, how did you get here? Got a horse?" Evans inquired.

"No, sir. I came here with my newlywed brother and his new wife. They are going to stay here until the wedding. Mother doesn't know they are married yet. After work today, I'm going to buy a horse," Shawn said.

"That's interesting. Bring them by. I'd like to meet them," Evans said.

Shawn spent the day touring his new work place, led by Evans. He also ran into Lewis, Wilson, and Cummings and was introduced to other Rangers he would be working with, Bob O'Leary, Dick Smith, and Jim Kline. He liked all of them.

It was five o'clock before he realized it.

Patrick and Patricia were waiting for him in the buggy, so he invited them in to meet Paul Evans.

Evans first words were to Patricia, "Young lady, don't I know you? You look familiar."

"Yes, sir. I met you once at the armory in Dallas," she replied.

"Of course. You are Chargin' Charlie's daughter, Patricia. Does your daddy know you ran off and got married?" Evans asked her.

"Not yet, but he will as soon as he gets the letter I wrote him. He is out in West Texas fighting Comanches," she replied.

Then Evans shook hands with Patrick and told him, "You are a lucky young man. Congratulations, and take good care of her or Chargin' Charlie will kill you," Evans warned him.

"Yes, sir. I am aware of that. I served under him in liberating Fort Stockton and running the Yankees out of East Texas, before I was wounded," Patrick answered.

"Well, I'm sure it will work out. Now see if you can go find a horse for Shawn. You can't be riding him into a fight in this buggy," Evans told him.

Patricia was dying to tell Shawn about the house they rented, but Evans was such a dominating figure, she hadn't had a chance to tell him about it.

"Oh, Shawn, we rented the loveliest little house for us. It has two bedrooms, a complete kitchen, a nice parlor, and a big porch. And the rent is only $10 a month. I am just so eager to show it to you. And I so hope you like it," she said.

"I sure want to see it, but first I have to find some place I can buy a horse and saddle," Shawn explained.

Patrick reported, "We saw a stable this morning. I think I can find it again, and I'll take you there now."

They found the stable, and Shawn went in and met Billy Burke, who owned the business.

"I'm looking to buy a good horse and a used saddle," Shawn said.

"Sir, you one of these new Texas Rangers?" Burke asked him.

"Yes, sir. I am," Shawn replied.

"Then, howdy. I'll make you a good deal. Come over here and look at this black stallion. He's a little frisky, but I think you're man enough to handle him. I've been asking $20 for him, but you can have him for $15, and I'll throw in a saddle and blanket," he offered.

"It's a deal. Saddle him up, and I'll ride him home," Shawn said. He paid him and Burke gave him a bridle, too.

Shawn followed Patrick and Patricia in the buggy to his new home. He found a small stable in the back. It would hold the two horses, but the buggy would have to sit outside. He also found some oats and hay the previous tenant left behind, so they could feed the horses without making a trip to the feed store.

Inside Patricia took Shawn by the hand and led him from room to room, anxious to show him the house they had picked out for him.

The next morning Shawn rode off to work. Patrick and Patricia would spend the day buying household necessities like pots and pans as well as towels and sheets.

At the Ranger station, Shawn learned he would be partnered with Sam Cummings. He already considered him a good friend from their days together in the army. Their first assignment was to ride to Floresville and bring back a prisoner they were holding there. His name was Craig Smith, and they wanted him in San Antonio for theft. The dumb bastard stole two horses from the stable in back of the Ranger station. The sheriff in Floresville recognized the brands on the horses and arrested Smith for theft. After the prisoner was signed for, they put shackles on him and put him on one of the horses. Cummings rode ahead to hold the reins to Smith's horse, and Shawn followed them on his horse.

Smith was a mere kid, probably a first offender. Maybe Judge Atkins would spare him a hanging because of his youth, but he had committed a hanging offense.

The trip home was uneventful, mostly because the Smith kid was scared to death.

Every evening when he got home, Patricia had a good meal waiting for him. She was a good cook.

Shawn's next assignment was not as routine as the first one.

Shawn, Cummings, Wilson, and Lewis were assigned to track down and kill or capture three men who robbed a stagecoach in Selma and killed the driver, guard, and two passengers. Shawn led the pack horse, and the three others rode quickly to Selma where they were met by Deputy Sheriff Ron Keim. Wilson was a good tracker and quickly found the bandits' tracks leading off to the west. Wilson pointed to one of the tracks which showed one of the horses had a broken shoe, missing a part of the rear shoe.

They tracked the gang until dark, then made camp, ate, got into bedrolls early, and were up before dawn drinking coffee and eating biscuits. When the sun came up they were already on the trail of their prey. By mid-afternoon, they found that the tracks led them directly to a small log cabin. Smoke was coming from the cabin's chimney, so they surrounded the cabin, and Wilson ordered them, "You in the cabin, you are surrounded by Texas Rangers. Come out with your hands raised, and we will let you live. Otherwise we will kill you."

His command was met by rifle fire coming from three different windows. Wilson had to jump for cover to keep from being killed.

The Rangers had their answer, so they all returned fire at once, causing the firing to stop, at least temporarily.

Lewis crawled to a side of the cabin, unseen. He then crawled underneath the window's line of sight, stood up close to one side of a window, and shot and killed the man who was going to resume shooting from the window. The other Rangers lined up on the other two windows, laying down a barrage of gunfire. It would be hard to survive near the two windows.

Lewis then proceeded to the door, shoved it open, threw

himself inside, and killed one of the two bandits still alive. The third bandit surrendered, coming out of the cabin unarmed, with his hands high above his head and shouting, "Don't shoot, Rangers. I give up."

Deputy Keim put manacles on him. When searching the cabin, they found the stage's strong box unopened, along with jewelry stolen from the woman they killed in the stage. They also found another shotgun marked "Wells Fargo" and a pouch of mail. The two bodies tied to their horses, the one prisoner on his horse, and the recovered loot on the back horse, the four Rangers and one deputy were a strange sight heading back to Selma. They arrived there the evening of the second day and met with Sheriff John Bishop. He identified the live prisoner as Sammy Simmons, and the dead men as his brothers.

Sheriff Bishop told them, "Congratulations, men. We have been looking for this gang for some time. They are wanted for murder, rape, highway robbery, and burglary."

Then he looked at the prisoner, and told him, "Son, you might as well have died with your brothers. Now I'm going to have to hang you right after the trial."

Sheriff Bishop wrote them a receipt for the prisoner, the bodies, and the recovered loot, and the Rangers rode off for home.

Major Evans also congratulated his men then told Shawn, "I'm glad you're back. Your brother told me your mother is being married next week, so let me know when you have to leave, and I'll make arrangements to give you time off."

Shawn replied, "Thank you, sir," and rode of for home.

Arriving there, Patricia gave him a warm welcome and Patrick told him, "Mama's wedding is a week from Saturday, so I think we had better leave here no later than next Thursday so we will be there in time."

Patricia added, "Now you boys fix yourselves a drink while I fix us all something to eat, then we both want to hear all about your trip."

Patricia quickly fixed fried steaks, potatoes, and biscuits. Shawn ate hungrily; glad to put something in his stomach other than the trail food he had eaten the past five days.

After dinner, Shawn related the details of his last trip.

Patricia commented, "What an exciting job you have."

"Yeah, but dangerous," Patrick added. Then Shawn noticed all of the purchases Patricia had made for his new home: two oil lamps, an entire kitchen full of skillets, pots, pans, and silverware. He commented, "Thank you, Patricia, but I feel like I should repay you for all of these things."

"You're welcome, but just consider the cost of these things as your first share of the profits from the boarding house," Patricia told him.

"Oh no, I don't want any share in that. The profits from the boarding house should be all yours, and the other boys'," Shawn corrected her.

"We'll talk about that later," Patricia said.

Then Patricia said, "After you get back, you're going to need a housekeeper. Want me to ask Conchita if she wants the job?"

"No, thanks. I'm not up to that just yet. I'll hire someone when I get back here from the wedding," Shawn told her. They all laughed.

Shawn was granted ten days unpaid leave. Patrick and Patricia had packed their clothes, and the three of them arrived in Dallas late Thursday afternoon. Shawn's horse, Negra

(Spanish for black), made the trip tied to the back of the buggy. Patricia stayed in the buggy while Patrick and Shawn went to see their mother at the apartment. Anna was not home, but they learned from their brothers that the boarding house was filled up. There were a lot of out-of-town guests coming into Dallas for the wedding. Disappointed but undaunted, they joined Patricia and rode to the Dallas Palace in hopes of seeing J.B. Rich.

He was glad to see them, and after they explained that Patrick and Patricia were married, he invited all of them to stay at his home. They swore him to secrecy about their wedding, still hoping to surprise their mother after her own wedding. He agreed and gave them directions to his house and invited Patrick and Shawn to his bachelor party to be held at the Dallas Palace Friday night. Patricia told Patrick she could spend that time with Conchita and invite her to attend the wedding as Shawn's date. Following Rich's directions, they pulled up in front of what Rich had described as his modest home.

Patricia uttered, "In a pig's eye it's a modest home; this is a mansion."

Rich's home, and soon to be home for their mother, was a three-story brick house in Arlington Heights, an affluent neighborhood of Dallas.

Patrick knocked on the door and it was answered by a middle-aged lady, who introduced herself as Lupe. Patrick told her who he was and told her of J.B.'s invitation.

"Come in, young man, and bring your two friends with you. I will get your room ready for you."

Patrick explained, "I'm afraid we will need two rooms. This is my wife, Patricia, and this is my brother Shawn."

"That will be absolutely no problem. We have four guest rooms. I will prepare two of them for you. Please wait in the parlor, and I will tell you when they are ready," Lupe said.

Soon the rooms were ready, and they all were settled in when J.B. arrived.

Learning he was home, they hurried down to meet him.

Patricia said, "Mr. Rich, you have a lovely home. Thank you for inviting us to stay here."

"You are all more than welcome. After all, in two days you will all be family, and you are welcome here anytime."

They were all seated in the parlor enjoying the margaritas Rich had fixed for them when Shawn boldly said, "J.B. you never talk about yourself. Is there anything you care to share with us about yourself?"

"I don't want to bore you, but I'll tell you if you are really interested," Rich said. "I am the son of Jewish Russian immigrants, Ivan and Anna Stepanovich. They landed in Galveston 50 years ago. My father, to feel more like an American, changed our name to Rich. He was a tailor and my mother was a seamstress. They made a decent living in Galveston, but decided they could do better in a large city, so they moved to Houston. My dad was a fine tailor, as had been his father, so business flourished.

"I was born first, and then two years later, my sister Catherine came along. I was the healthy one, but poor Catherine was sickly and died at only four years old. Her death grieved our mother so much. She died of grief only five years later. My dad was also grief-stricken, but knowing he had to care for me, he carried on and continued to prosper. He died when I was 20 years old. I had a little money he left me but didn't know what to do with it. I drifted around for a while, then finally arrived here in Dallas. I got lucky and met some friends who also had some money to invest. Their names are Jim Stock and Ben Dooley, and they are still my partners. I had always dreamed of owning a fancy gambling casino and finally came up with the idea of opening up the Dallas Palace. Some of my friends also were interested, so they invested too, and we opened up the place. At first we had a hard time of it, but gradually word spread that we had an honest operation, and in a few years we became a success."

"Wow, that's some story," Patrick said.

"Well, it's all true," J.B. explained.

"What does 'J.B.' stand for?" Patricia wanted to know.

"OK, if you promise not to laugh, I'll tell you," he said.

"We promise," they all answered in unison.

"Well, my dad was an avid reader, and he read everything he could find about the founding of America and its early history. His hero became Daniel Boone, but he was afraid people would laugh at me with that name. He thought of naming me Jacob Boone, but said that sounded too Jewish, so he named me John Boone, which I shortened to J.B. And that's the story," J.B. explained.

Then dinner was served, and all three of the young people ate with a greater respect for J.B. Rich.

After dinner, J.B. invited them into his library, and Lupe served them coffee and brandy. Patrick thought, *Boy, Mama sure found her a good husband.*

The next morning J.B. left for the Dallas Palace to get everything ready for the lunch crowd and to prepare the room for the bachelor party that night and the wedding tomorrow morning.

Patricia left for the armory to see Conchita, and the boys left for the boarding house to visit their mother and brothers.

When she saw them she said, "I'm sorry I missed you yesterday and didn't have a room for you. Where did you stay?"

"With J.B.," Patrick replied.

They spent the afternoon visiting until Patrick and Shawn left to get ready for the bachelor party. Joseph and Mark asked Anna why they couldn't go to the bachelor party, and she told them, "Don't try and grow up too fast. All of that will come later on."

At the party the boys met a lot of Rich's business partners and friends. His partners were Jim Stock, a banker, and Ben Dooley, who owned several grocery stores.

Patrick was also pleased to see Charles Goodnight, his old boss during the cattle drive. Goodnight introduced him to Oliver Loving, his partner in the cattle business. Goodnight also told Patrick that he and Loving intended to drive a herd of cattle from Texas to Montana and establish a herd there.

Both boys' heads were swimming because of meeting so many other important people. They met Jim Welch, Lieutenant Governor of Texas; George Hansen, mayor of Dallas; and Paul Lowe, mayor of Houston. Shawn whispered to Patrick, "Wow, J.B. sure knows a lot of big shots."

"Sure does," Patrick answered.

Then J.B., instead of making a traditional speech, told them all, "Thanks for coming. Please have a good time in celebrating my last night as a bachelor. And if you haven't yet met my future stepsons, Patrick and Shawn Sweeney, please look them up. Raise your hands, boys, so they can find you."

Patrick and Shawn obeyed, and got a round of applause.

By eleven o'clock, when everyone had their fill of food and drink, the party broke up.

J.B. and the boys returned to J.B.'s house where Patricia was waiting for them. They all immediately went to bed, anxious to get up early to get ready for the wedding, which was to happen at eleven.

# CHAPTER 16

⚬꧁ ꧂⚬

# THE HUGE WEDDING
## OF ANNA AND J.B.

The wedding was not only beautiful and well done; it was filled with surprises. All of the guests were surprised by how beautiful Anna looked. At middle-age, she was as beautiful as a very young woman. Having five children had not ruined the hourglass figure she displayed when young. Over the years she had gained some weight, but it was distributed evenly over her frame. The rose-colored dress she wore blended with her white complexion. The few strands of gray hair only added to her youthful appearance, not detracted from it.

Her husband-to-be described her wonderfully. "You look absolutely stunning," he said.

The next surprise was for Anna when she saw her boys in their blazers that Rich secretly bought for them.

She was also surprised to see all of her sons with dates: Patrick with Patricia; Shawn with Conchita; and Mark and Joseph with two sisters, Pam and Linda Macauley. At first glance she thought they might be twins, but later would learn they were only sisters who resembled each other a lot. She made a mental note to find out more about them after the ceremony.

Her next surprise came when she looked closely at J.B. His coal-black hair was combed to perfection, and his perfectly trimmed mustache enhanced his facial features. The graying hair around his temples only added to his distinguished-looking appearance. His tall stature was perfectly fitted into the black tuxedo he wore.

Father Lynch had done his part to prepare a long table covered with a white linen cloth that would serve as an altar, and two of the men from church had moved in two kneeling benches for the bride and groom. He started the ceremony by saying, "Over the years I have performed many marriages, but none that made me as happy as joining these two people in holy matrimony. I have known both of them for many years and wondered how long it would take for them to love each other."

Patrick accompanied his mother up to the altar, shook hands with Rich, and delivered her to him.

Jim Welch was chosen to be J.B.'s best man. Before he was Lieutenant Governor, he was an attorney and was J.B.'s first partner in the Dallas Palace. Anna had Betsy Weston stand with her. Father Lynch said several prayers in Latin, while J.B. and Anna knelt. Then they gathered together. They exchanged vows, then J.B. put the ring on Anna's finger. Father Lynch sprinkled them with holy water and pronounced them man and wife. They kissed.

J.B. jokingly told Anna he got wet from the holy water.

Anna replied, "Don't worry; it doesn't burn holes in Jews." They laughed.

Then J.B. and Anna led the group into the main ballroom. One table was set up as an open bar, and one table set up with food of all shapes and descriptions. Anna and J.B. were mobbed by well- wishers. Then Anna sought out her sons who each gave her hugs and kisses.

Patrick gave her his surprise when he introduced Patricia as his wife. Anna looked as if she might faint, but Patrick continued telling her, "Mama, we didn't tell you because we didn't want to upstage your wedding."

Anna said, "And I suppose you had some judge somewhere marry you."

"No, Mama—Father Lynch married us in his church," Patricia told her.

"Why, you little devils. Well, I love you both and I am happy for you," Anna said and kissed both of them.

Then Anna made a point of talking to Mark and Joseph. "Introduce me to your girlfriends," she commanded.

Mark spoke first, "Mama, this is Pam Macauley. She and I have been seeing each other for some time."

Then her sister Linda spoke up, "It is nice to meet you, Mrs. Rich. My name is Linda Macauley, and Joseph and I like each other a lot."

Anna then told them, "Nice to meet you both. I hope my boys will be good to you. When we get back from the honeymoon, please come and see me, and we will get better acquainted."

J.B. had been silent, just listening, then told Anna, "I know their parents, Doris and William. They are very well to do. Years ago William started working as a saddle maker. His work was so good, the demand for his saddles increased tremendously, and he could demand a premium for his work. Now he employs four full-time assistants who create his saddles for him. He hand-picked and trained each one of them and closely supervises and inspects each saddle. Now he heads up one of the fastest growing businesses in Dallas."

"Then I'm surprised they would take up with my boys," Anna answered.

Their conversation was interrupted by more well-wishers. The party was getting louder, and Jim Welch suggested they leave to catch the train for New Orleans for a week-long honeymoon. Holding hands like two teenagers, they left with Welch for the train.

Then the four Sweeney boys and their girls found a corner table where they all could get better acquainted. Patrick began, "Well, I'm glad Mama didn't have a heart attack tonight. We all sure laid some surprises on her."

Pam then said, "I don't think after all she has been through in life that any of us could surprise her with our news."

"I think you're right," Patricia agreed. They all spent the next hour talking and getting acquainted until Patricia reminded everyone, "It is getting late. I think we had better all be getting home."

Joseph and Mark took their dates home. The buggy only had three seats, but that didn't bother Shawn and Conchita. She sat on his lap, wrapped around him like a tightly wrapped bandage. There were no complaints out of Shawn. Patrick drove to Conchita's dad's apartment, and she kissed Shawn good-night, told Patrick and Patricia good-night, then bolted for her door. The rest of them left for the boarding house to get settled in. When they put the horse away in the carriage house, they saw the other buggy and knew the other boys had beaten them home.

They decided Patrick and Patricia would take their mother's room, Shawn, a room by himself, and Mark and John shared the third room until Shawn had to leave.

The next day was Sunday. Patricia fixed breakfast for everyone, then they left for 10 a.m. mass. Mark and Joseph had agreed to meet Pam and Linda there, and they were waiting for them on the church steps.

When Father Lynch saw them all coming in together, he got a huge smile on his face. He had baptized every one of them. During mass Patrick took time to have a closer look at the two Macauley girls. They could be mistaken for twins unless they were studied carefully. Both girls had pretty rounded faces with carefully groomed black hair and matching black eyes.

Pam was a little more developed than Linda, probably because she was three years older. They both had nice bodies, pretty legs, and beautiful white skin. Mark and Joseph had picked well for themselves.

When mass was over, Father Lynch greeted parishioners as they left, as was his custom. The Sweeneys approached him. Patrick asked him, "Father, our mother's old cook and housekeeper both quit. They wanted to retire, and now we wondered if you might know of someone who might be interested in these jobs?"

Father Lynch raised his eyes to heaven and said, "Thank you, dear God, for solving the problem I have been praying for."

Everyone looked puzzled, so Father Lynch continued, "I

have these two ladies who have a problem. Mary Martin and her sister Mabel are living together with no means of support since Mary's husband was killed during the war. They asked me if I could help, and I asked God to help me help them. Now my prayers may have been answered if you will hire them. They are both excellent cooks, good housekeepers, and as honest as the day is long. I will see them after the noon mass, and I'll send them to see you if you are going to be at the boarding house."

"Thank you, Father. We will make a point of being there," Patrick assured him.

Shawn offered to treat everyone to breakfast, so they all met at the diner. They did rush breakfast slightly so they would be home for sure when Mary and Mabel came to see them. After breakfast Mark and Joseph took their dates to the park, Shawn rode to see if he could find Conchita, and Patrick and Patricia rode home to wait on Mary and Mabel Martin.

All of the guests had checked out. Most of them had checked in for the wedding so now had gone home. All of the linens needed to be changed and laundered, all of the rooms cleaned, and the hall swept.

Patricia was dreading having to do it herself, so she was delighted when the sisters arrived for the interview.

After the interview, more prayers than Father Lynch's were answered. Mary and Mabel found a job. Patricia and Patrick had two good employees. God answers prayers; you have only to ask Him.

Within a week things were running smoothly at the boarding house. Guests were bragging about Mary's cooking, and Mabel kept the rooms spotlessly clean. J.B. and Anna returned home from their honeymoon just in time to see Shawn before he had to return to San Antonio. Shawn reluctantly rode back to San Antonio, wishing he didn't have to go. He would miss his family and Conchita, who had really captured his fancy.

## CHAPTER 17

# SHAWN'S ADVENTURE IN LAREDO

S hawn returned to the Ranger station and had little time to relax. He, Wilson, Lewis, and Cummings were ordered to leave the next morning for Laredo. Paul Evans explained that a group of banditos were crossing the river, robbing, raping, and murdering in the Laredo area, then crossing back into Mexico, where they find the safety of their home.

Evans said, "I'm going to give you an order I will deny ever giving you. Find those bastards and kill them. If you are chasing them and they cross the river into Mexico, take off your badges and go after them."

Jack Wilson was more experienced than the others, so he said, "What order, sir? We didn't hear any order." Everyone smiled.

There was a stagecoach to Laredo, but the Rangers elected to ride there, with a pack horse and supplies, and be ready to start to seek out the banditos. They rode on the stage road because it was easier traveling than riding cross-country.

Once they had to move fast to get off of the road to avoid being run over by the fast moving stage coach pulled by six horses. Several passengers, as well as the driver and shotgun guard, gave them friendly waves as they passed.

Another advantage of using this road was that they could overnight at the stagecoach stop and sleep in a good bed, instead of camping out. For a very minimal fee they slept, ate two meals, and had their horses tended to. The friendly married couple who managed the stop also fixed them sandwiches to take along for their trip. They reached the outskirts of Laredo and found a rooming house they could use for a headquarters during their stay there. To conserve their money, they rented one room with two double beds for as long as they were there. The rooming house did not serve food, but the landlady directed them to a nearby diner where they could have breakfast.

They all ate a hearty breakfast, knowing it would have to stave off hunger until dinnertime tonight. After they ate, they rode to the sheriff's office to let him know they were in the area and to inquire about recent bandito activity in the area. They learned the last report he had was from the Hogan ranch, about three miles north of town. Three days before, they killed Paul and Alma Hogan and carried off their daughter, Elena. The sheriff explained he did not have the manpower to patrol the whole county. He had his hands full just keeping peace in the wild town Laredo had become.

Hearing this, the Rangers rode off for the Hogan ranch, hoping to pick up the trail of the banditos, even if it was three days old. Wilson thought their chances were good at finding signs because there had been no rain in the area.

When they reached the ranch they found the partially burned ranch house, two fresh graves, and a barn completely emptied of livestock.

Wilson dismounted, walked around the site, then returned, saying, "There were ten of the sons a bitches. They drove the horses and cattle off in that direction," pointing to the west.

Cummings remarked, "Then let's get after them. They can't move very fast driving all of that livestock."

They followed the tracks west, then north. Wilson told them, "The bastards were headed north looking for some place to ford the river."

The terrain was getting more rocky, but all of that livestock left so many tracks they were able to track them easily.

Darkness was approaching so the Rangers made camp for the night. They built only a small fire that could not be seen from far off. They ate beans and stale biscuits, slept on their bedrolls, and were up at dawn, anxious to get back on the trail of the banditos. After another hour of tracking the slow moving banditos and their herd of horses and cattle, they found a shallow place where their prey had crossed the river.

Wilson told the others, "I'm going across and will see if I can find them. You stay here because I can make better time riding alone. If I'm not back in two hours come and look for me."

Wilson was the ranking Ranger, so the rest of them followed

orders. Taking off his badge and putting it in his shirt pocket, Wilson crossed the river and disappeared into the cottonwood trees on the Mexican side of the Rio Grande.

The other three Rangers waited anxiously, but they had less than an hour to wait.

At first they heard only distant gunfire, but the firing became louder, and then they saw Wilson riding for his life. He was riding hard, reigns in his teeth, and firing his pistol with his only arm. He was being closely pursued by eight Mexicans, all shooting wildly and screaming curses at Wilson.

When they were close enough, the Rangers fired on the pursuers. For the first time, Shawn was able to see Lefty Lewis' famous fast draw. Lewis drew his pistol and fired three shots, downing two of the pursuers, before the other Rangers had a chance to draw their pistols. Shawn and Cummings also started shooting and each downed one of the Mexicans. Lewis fired again and killed another one of them. Wilson then wheeled around and killed one more of them.

The two remaining banditos attempted to ride away, but rifle shots from Shawn and Cummings killed them.

Then the rest of the Rangers crossed the river to aid Wilson.

Lewis finished off the wounded Mexicans with a shot to the head.

Then Shawn noticed blood dripping from Wilson's left leg. He told him he had better get to a doctor. Instead, Wilson put a tourniquet around his leg and said to the group, "There's two more of them who stayed with the herd. Let's go kill them and see if we can rescue that poor girl they took."

They counted on the herd guards thinking they were their

returning friends and could get close enough to shoot them before they realized it was not their friends returning.

The two guards were surprised when the riders were not friends, but Rangers who were shooting at them.

Both men went down, both having taken bullets from the Rangers' guns. One was dead, and Lewis went to talk to the wounded one. Taking the Mexican's gun, he asked him, "Where is the girl you kidnapped?"

*"No hablo ingles,"* the Mexican replied.

In his best Spanish, Lewis asked him, *"Donde esta pequita senorita?"*

*"Muerta,"* was the reply.

"You mean dead because you bastards raped and murdered her," Lewis said, his anger showing in his eyes.

The Mexican understood this, and he also understood he was about to die, so he said, *"No mi. Los otros."*

"Others my ass," Lewis said and shot the Mexican between the eyes.

Cummings took charge, with Lewis wounded, and said, "Shawn, you take Jack into Laredo, *muy pronto,* and get him to a doctor. Ride like hell, and take two of these stolen horses as spares so you can move fast. We will gather up the weapons and the rest of the horses, and follow you later."

"What about the cattle?" Lewis asked.

"We'll have to leave them here. There is plenty of graze and water, so they will be fine until someone finds them," Cummings said.

"What about the dead ones?" Lewis wanted to know.

"To hell with them. The coyotes have to eat too," came the answer.

Shawn and Wilson left in a gallop, each leading a spare horse. When their mounts became tired, they began riding the spare horses and leading the tired ones.

When they reached Laredo, Shawn asked the first man he saw, "Where can we find a doctor? My friend is wounded."

"Two streets ahead on the right," the man replied.

They pulled up at a small house. The shingle hanging in front read: "Doctor Luther Williams, M.D."

Shawn knocked on the door and was admitted by a young woman. He told her, "We are Texas Rangers, and my friend here is wounded in the leg. Can we see the doctor?"

"I'll get him for you right away. He is examining a woman with gout, but this will take priority," she said.

Dr. Williams ushered out the lady with gout. She limped to a chair, sat down, and asked, "Are you Texas Rangers?"

"Yes ma'am," Shawn answered.

Then Shawn helped Wilson get into the examining room, where Dr. Williams helped Jack take off his jeans and boots, then examined the wound. Wilson obviously was in pain, so the doctor asked him, "Want a drink?"

"I never turn down a drink," Wilson said.

The doctor poured him a half-glass of brandy, which he instantly emptied.

"Thanks, Doc," he said.

The doctor probed about the leg, and then announced, "Well, it looks like you got lucky. The bullet missed the bone, but you have lost a lot of blood. Do you have a place you can stay off your feet for a day or two?" Dr. Williams asked.

Shawn answered for him, "We are staying at a rooming

house up the street. There are two more of us, and we can look after him."

"That's good. Now if you will wait in the outer room and ask my nurse to come in here, I'll get him bandaged up and you can take him home with you," Dr. Williams instructed.

Shawn went out and asked the nurse to go in to help the doctor.

Then he took a seat opposite the gout-stricken lady.

She asked him, "How did your friend get shot?"

"We got into a shootout with some banditos up river from here," he told her.

"Were they the same ones who raided the Hogan Ranch?"

"I think so. We tracked them from the Hogan Ranch to where we caught up with them," he said.

"Did you find the little Hogan girl?" she wanted to know.

"No, ma'am. I'm afraid they killed her," he replied.

"Oh, that poor thing. I hope you killed them all," she said.

"Yes ma'am. We did," he answered.

"Good. I am Mrs. Garcia, and I was that poor little girl's godmother. My husband is the mayor here, so if there is anything you need while you are here, just let me know," she told him.

Then the doctor and nurse came out and asked Mrs. Garcia, "That Ranger is sleeping now, and I don't want to wake him, so could I see you tomorrow?"

"Of course. Let that poor man sleep. His partner here just told me he was shot during a gunfight with the bandits who killed the Hogans. They are heroes in this town," she announced.

Then the doctor got interested and asked, "How many banditos were there?"

"Ten," Shawn responded.

"And how many of you Rangers?" he inquired.

"Four," answered Shawn.

"Then you are heroes," the nurse chimed in.

"No, not heroes, just Texas Rangers doing our job," Shawn replied.

"Where are you staying?" Mrs. Garcia asked.

"At the rooming house down the street, next to the diner," Shawn responded.

"Well, we can do better than that for heroes. Blanca, run over to the Laredo house and see if they have two rooms available for our heroes," she instructed.

The nurse, who obviously was named Blanca, ran out the door and returned a few minutes later saying, "Yes ma'am they have two nice rooms available."

"Well, when that poor man wakes up help his friend here, get him over there, and tell the hotel to send me the bill," Mrs. Garcia instructed her. It was obvious Mrs. Garcia was used to giving orders and having them obeyed.

Mrs. Garcia left, and Shawn thanked her for her kindness.

The doctor went back in to check on Wilson, and Shawn spent the time talking with the nurse. "My name is Shawn Sweeney, and you must be Blanca."

"*Si*, I am Blanca Rodriguez, and it is nice to know you. I've never met a Texas Ranger before," she told him.

As she was talking, Shawn studied her carefully. She was a petite, light brown-skinned Mexican, but with blonde hair and blue eyes. She had a nice figure with large breasts. She had nicely shaped legs sticking out from her clean white uniform.

*She is cute,* he thought.

Wilson was still sleeping when Lewis and Cummings came into the office. Cummings said, "We saw your horses outside and thought you would be here. How is Jack?"

"He is sleeping, but will be fine after a few days of rest and changing the bandages," Shawn replied.

Then Shawn introduced them to nurse Rodriguez and the doctor. Then Dr. Williams asked them, "Do any of you know how he lost his right arm?"

They all shook their heads no.

"Well, he told me just before he went to sleep. He took a minnie ball in his arm at Antietam. He said it was a wound very similar to what he has in his leg. His arm wasn't tended to properly, and he got gangrene, and they had to cut it off. We sure don't want that to happen to his leg, or he will be in bad shape. I want to examine him every day for three days, and I'll send Blanca to the hotel twice a day to change his bandages. When he wakes up, use my stretcher to carry him over to the hotel. Then I'll come by in the morning to have a look at him," the doctor told them.

Cummings left to make out a report for the sheriff and to send a telegram to Tall Paul.

The wire read:

> *To Major Paul Evans—San Antonio*
> *Job finished here. Ten banditos dead. Jack Wilson severely wounded in leg. Doctor in Laredo says should not be moved or use leg for three days. Reply*

> *to Laredo House where we are staying courtesy of*
> *Laredo mayor. Advise how to proceed.*
>
> > *Sam Cummings*

Then he wrote a full report and delivered it to the sheriff's office. He rode back to the doctor's office and helped move Wilson on a stretcher to the hotel. There they found luxurious rooms, far better than anything they had ever stayed in. They put Lewis in one room with Shawn, and Sam and Lefty shared an adjoining room.

The next morning Dr. Williams and his nurse came to check on Lewis. The doctor looked at the wound and announced there was no evidence of infection, then applied more salve to the wound and watched as Blanca deftly applied the bandages. Saying he would be by again tomorrow, he shook hands with Shawn. Blanca and Shawn also shook hands, as if neither of them wanted to let go. The doctor noticed, and said, "Let's go Blanca. We will both be back tomorrow."

Soon a wire from Paul Evans was delivered. It read:

> *Good work but sorry Jack so badly wounded. Stay*
> *put. I am sending O'Leary out there in my private*
> *buggy. It is smooth riding and has room in the back*
> *to make a bed for Jack. See you soon.*
>
> > *Evans*

Sam and Lefty went out for a few drinks, dinner, and to bring dinner home for Jack and Shawn. They also brought a bottle of rye whiskey to share.

That evening Sam unwrapped a package he brought with

him from the battle site. It contained the weapons he had collected from the dead banditos. Among the various guns was a pair of silver-plated, ivory-handled Colt Peacemakers in 45 caliber.

"Anyone want one of these?" he asked.

Lewis replied, "I don't. My pistol has a hair trigger just the way I like it. Give one to Jack, and the other one to the kid," he said, pointing to Shawn.

Jack and Shawn both replied, "Thanks."

Cummings told them, "Don't thank me. Those bastards probably killed someone to get them, but now they are back in honest hands."

The next day Blanca came in the morning and changed the bandages on Jack's wound. She told Shawn it looked good. Shawn looked forward to her visits so they could spend time talking together. She told him she came to San Antonio occasionally, so he wrote down the address of his house, and also the address of the Ranger station.

After the doctor visited that afternoon, he reported the wound was healing nicely with no sign of infection. He felt Jack could travel after Blanca changed the bandages the next morning.

Cummings tried to pay the doctor but was told, "The service you did for this community is payment enough. The entire town is indebted to you."

That evening Shawn and Lefty went to get supper for everyone and a bottle of whiskey. The dining room was located at the rear of the bar, and as they walked through the bar, a drunk standing there remarked, "Hey everyone, look at the big, tough Texas Rangers!"

Lefty was angered. "Just fill your mouth with more whiskey and keep it shut," he said.

The drunk fingered the handle of his pistol, but Shawn put his hand over the drunk's hand and told him, "Back off, mister. That is Lefty Lewis, and he could kill you before you even drew your pistol. I saw him draw and shoot three times, killing two men, before I could even get my pistol out."

The drunk's face grew somber, and Lefty and Shawn proceeded to the dining room. After they ate, they took chili and corn bread to Jack and Sam and a bottle of whiskey for them to share. As they left, they noticed the drunk's friends had done him a huge favor and taken him home.

Jack Wilson ate a lot for the first time in awhile, consuming two bowls of chili, three pieces of cornbread, and a large glass of whiskey. This was a good sign. He was feeling better. Late that evening O'Leary arrived with the buggy.

After Jack's bandages were changed the next morning, they got ready to leave. As the others used their bedrolls to make a comfortable bed for Jack in the buggy, Shawn hung back to talk with Blanca. She kissed him good-bye and promised to visit him when she came to San Antonio. With O'Leary driving the buggy, Cummings sitting beside him, and Wilson comfortable in his makeshift bed, they left for San Antonio. Lefty and Shawn led the string of horses. The *banditos'* horses would become part of the Ranger's stable.

They arrived in San Antonio very late the following day. It was almost midnight by the time they got Jack settled into bed in his room. Cummings volunteered to stay with him and Lefty and Shawn rode off to their homes, after stabling the horses at the Ranger's stable. The next morning Shawn and Lefty went to see Tall Paul. He told them they looked tired and to go home and rest. He was going to check on Jack, and would see them the next morning.

There were no assignments coming up, so all of the Rangers spent time with paperwork all week long.

# CHAPTER 18

ಀಀಀ

# THE SWEENEYS IN DALLAS

While Shawn was off to West Texas, things were rather boring. By comparison, in Dallas under the supervision of Patrick and Patricia, the boarding house flourished. The oil boom in Texas made a lot of new millionaires, and a vast majority of them spent money at the Dallas Palace. It was also prospering.

Mark and Joseph had moved in with their mother, and J.B. gave Patrick and Patricia the entire carriage house apartment to themselves.

Patricia had received a long letter from her father, which she and Patrick read and reread many times.

> *My Dear Patricia,*
> *I couldn't be more pleased that you and Patrick are married and happy together. I liked that young man from the first time I met him at the N.C.O. ball at Fort Stockton. As for me, I have been all over West Texas, New Mexico, and now Arizona. For months we have been chasing an Apache chief they*

call Cochise. He has over 500 braves, and they are as good as my horse soldiers. If they were as well armed as we are, they would have defeated us some time ago. Several times had we not had the Hotchkiss Mountain canon, they would have slaughtered us. They call that gun the Thunder Gun, and it scares the hell out of them.

It looks like things may be calming down here soon. I met a very remarkable young man named Tom Jeffords. Jeffords was once a scout for the Army and later was working as a supervisor for Pony Express. After some of his mail riders were killed by Apache raiding parties, Jeffords with more bravery than I could ever summon up rode into Cochise's camp under a flag of truce. Cochise was so impressed with the bravery of Jeffords, they met several more times and eventually Jeffords and Cochise became blood brothers.

Later President Grant sent General Oliver Howard to negotiate peace with the Apaches. Using Jeffords as an intermediate, General Howard was able to negotiate a treaty with Cochise. In return for peace, Cochise demanded his tribe could remain in the Chiricahua Mountains and Tom Jeffords be named Indian Agent. His demands were met and peace is now arriving in this region. If this treaty lasts, I may be able to take leave and see you soon.

Your loving father,
Charles

Reading this time after time, they both commented on how the difference one man can make can alter history. They both also read many times the letter Shawn wrote the family from Laredo, before the chase of the banditos began. After Anna reread the letter she commented, "He is doing a dangerous job. I hope he is working with some good men."

Patrick reassured her, "Oh, he is, Mama. Patricia and I both met a lot of them, and they are all very tough, capable men. He is in very good hands."

Patrick and Patricia were doing a very fine job of running the boarding house, but Anna came to visit at least once a week and always asked a lot of questions. She also sent Mark and Joseph by several times a week to help with the chores, like cleaning the stable and getting hay and oats for the visitors' horses.

"OK, I feel better about him, but I can't help but worry about all four of you boys," Anna said as she left to join J.B. for lunch at the Dallas Palace, a lunch they enjoyed together several times every week.

Shawn looked forward to the times Charles Goodnight came to stay at the boarding house. Despite all the money he made during the war, selling beef to the Confederate Army, he still insisted in staying in one of the smaller rooms.

During his next visit he was having coffee after breakfast and asked Patrick to join him.

"I'm putting together another cattle drive. I think I mentioned it to you before, but now Oliver Loving and I are making the final arrangements. We will probably be gone for two years. Want to be my head wrangler?" Goodnight asked.

"Thank you for asking me, sir, but I am married now and have to stick close to home," Patrick replied.

"Know any good men who might be interested? But tell them they have to understand we are going all the way to Montana. I intend to set up a ranch and establish a cattle breeding business there," Goodnight told him.

"My brothers Joseph or Mark might be interested. Joseph is 18 and Mark is 17, so if you want me to, I'll ask them."

"Are they as good at working horses as you?" Goodnight asked him.

"They both are as good as I am," Patrick replied.

"Better ask your Mama, too. I sure don't want her mad at me," Goodnight warned.

"Yes, sir. I will. How long will you be staying with us?" Patrick asked.

"Just this weekend, then I have to get back to the ranch," he replied.

"OK, sir. I will find out something for you before you leave," Patrick said.

Goodnight's offer caused surprise, tension, and confusion in the Sweeney family.

Before telling his mother, Patrick spoke with Mark and Joseph, offering them the job. Mark told him he would have to answer him the next day. He wanted to discuss it with Pam.

Joseph thought he might be interested, and would give him an answer after he talked it over with Linda.

Patrick was surprised at both answers. He did not realize the boys were so involved with their girlfriends; secretly though, he hoped they would both turn the offer down, because if they left he would have to take on more of the chores himself.

After his brothers left, Patrick told Patricia of the boys' responses and asked her opinion. She replied, "I think that was smart of both of them. I think they are both planning a future with those girls, and it is only fair they ask for their advice."

The next afternoon both brothers came to the boarding house with their answer. Mark said, "That is nice of Mr. Goodnight to think of us for a trip to Montana, but I'm afraid I can't accept. Pam's father has offered me the opportunity to learn his business from the ground up. Starting next Monday I will begin working for him as an apprentice saddle maker. It will take me at least two years to learn the trade. Pam agrees that would be the best future for the two of us."

This surprised both Patrick and Patricia, but they were more surprised by the answer they got from Joseph, "I am going to take the job. Linda and I both want to own a ranch someday, and I should be able to make enough money on this job to buy a small spread when I get back."

"Then she agrees you should take the job?" Patricia said.

"Yes, she does," Joseph answered.

"Well, I guess that's settled. Now we had better tell Mama and see what she says," Patrick advised them all.

The next day was Saturday, and Patrick arranged with J.B. for all of them to have lunch together at the Dallas Palace. Pam and Linda were also invited. After lunch Patrick told his mother that Mark and Joseph had some news for her. Her first response was, "Who is getting married?"

"No one, at least not right away," Patrick answered.

Mark, holding hands with Pam under the table, went first, "Mama, Pam's daddy has offered me a job as an apprentice saddle maker, to learn his business, and I am starting to work there Monday morning."

"Well, I think that is wonderful," she said.

Then Joseph spoke. "Mama, Mr. Goodnight wants me to be a horse wrangler on his cattle drive. He is going all the way to Montana, and I probably will be gone for two years."

Anna grew a little pale but said, "Well, you are a man now and able to make up your own mind. Linda, do you agree with this?"

Linda replied, "Yes, ma'am. We both want to have our own ranch someday, and Joseph thinks he can save enough money on the drive for us to buy one when he gets back. I only hope he comes home safely."

Anna's composure had returned and she commented, "I trust Charles Goodnight to protect Joseph. He sure brought Patrick home to me safe and sound."

Then J.B. spoke up, "Goodnight is one of the finest men I have ever known. If I had a son I would entrust him to go with Goodnight."

"Then it's all settled. Joseph and I will go see Mr. Goodnight tomorrow and tell him," Patrick said.

"Why not tell him now? There he is, over there having lunch at that far table," J.B. interjected.

Patrick and Joseph left to tell Goodnight. Seeing them coming, he invited them to sit with him as he finished his coffee.

"I hope you have good news for me," he said.

Joseph said, "I hope you think it is good news. I would like to join you on the cattle drive. My brother Mark has already taken another job, but I am just as good a wrangler as he is."

"I'm sure you are. I saw you sitting with a young lady. Does she approve of you leaving her for two years?"

"Yes, sir. She does. We will be saving to buy a ranch, and what I make on the drive can get us a nest egg," Joseph answered him.

"Know how to use a Colt and a Winchester?" Goodnight asked.

"He doesn't yet, but I will teach him before you are ready to leave," Patrick told him.

"Fine. You're hired. I will see you before we leave in two months. Now let's go say hello to your mother and J.B., and you can introduce me to your girlfriends," he said. As they approached the table J.B. stood up, shook hands with Charles, and introduced him to the group.

Anna said to Charles, "Well, I understand you're taking away another of my sons. I just want you to know I hope you will bring him home safe to me, as you did with Patrick."

"You can be sure I will. I wouldn't want to have your Irish temper unleashed on me if anything happened to him," Charles said.

Everyone at the table laughed, including Anna.

After meeting Mark and the two girls, Charles took his leave and returned to the boarding house.

"He is a nice man," Linda remarked.

Pam added, "He is an imposing figure of a man. I pity the person who crosses him."

Patrick agreed, "Believe it. I have seen him riled up, and I always pitied the person who did the riling."

Patrick spoke next, "I hate to lose my two helpers, because that means more work for me."

J.B. offered a suggestion, "Why don't you add a little class to the place and hire a stable hand? That way you could offer attended livery. He could take the guests' horses when they arrive and take care of the horses."

Anna added, "That's an excellent idea, J.B. They can certainly afford it because the boarding house is doing so well."

"Thanks, I'll start looking for someone right away," Patrick told them.

True to his word, he started asking all over town for a stable hand. The recent oil boom had employed a lot of men, leaving few who would work as a stable hand. One day however he was approached by a very large black man, who introduced himself as Leo Lincoln. He asked, "Is that job takin' care of horses still open?"

When told that it was, he continued, "Well, suh, when I was a slave, I took care of my mastah's horses, and I be good at it. I know I be only half smart, but I'm a good worker. You see."

"Then I'll give you a try. I'll pay you $1 a day, and you can fix yourself a room in the carriage house tack room, and you can take your meals in the kitchen with Mary and Mabel," Patrick said.

"That be fine with me," Leo said, and they shook hands.

Now relieved of the stable chores, Patrick was able to spend time with Joseph teaching him how to use the Winchester rifle and Colt pistol. Patrick gave Joseph his old Winchester but wouldn't part with his Colt, so Joseph bought his own pistol, a used Remington top break revolver in .44 Russian caliber. He had to pay $4, it but it was in good condition and the gun shop owner threw in a holster and a belt. After Joseph also purchased two boxes of cartridges, the owner also gave him a bowie knife and sheath.

After practicing in the open country several times, Joseph became proficient with the use of both weapons. Time passed quickly and Joseph now had to leave to join the cattle drive.

# CHAPTER 19

### ❧❧ ❧❧

# SHAWN'S ADVENTURES CONTINUE WITH THE RANGERS

Since their last exciting assignment in Laredo, things had been relatively quiet at the San Antonio Ranger station. Paul Evans had received a telegram from the mayor of Floresville. A sheriff there had gone bad and was stealing land from the local ranchers. He sometimes kidnapped a member of a local family and held them for ransom. The ranch owner was forced to sign over the deed to his ranch at a greatly reduced price to have their family member returned safely.

Shawn and Lefty rode out there to check out the mayor's allegations.

It was a hard two-day's ride, and upon reaching Floresville, they went to the mayor's office. There they met Mayor Bill Myers. He told them, "Thank you for coming, but you may be too late. The latest victim of Sheriff Bradshaw became so enraged, he formed a group of vigilantes, and now they have Bradshaw and his two crooked deputies surrounded in his house. They are threatening to burn him out if he does not surrender."

Mayor Myers directed them to the sheriff's house, and the two rangers rode there. When they arrived, they found the men all around the house. They looked up at the leader, Tom Timmons. He told them, "That no good son of a bitch Bradshaw took my 16-year-old daughter and wanted me to deed over my ranch for $500. It is worth ten times that. I love my daughter so agreed to it. I did get my young daughter back, but they raped her. I told myself, enough is enough, so I asked my friends here to help me get the bastards. A few of them had also been victimized by Bradshaw, so they were eager to help."

Lefty and Shawn had heard enough, so they took shelter behind an overturned wagon, and Lefty shouted into the house.

"Attention in the house. This is Texas Rangers Lewis and Sweeney. We came here to arrest you, but now it looks like we are going to save your life. Throw down your weapons and come out with your hands in the air, or I'll unleash this mob on you."

The answer came in the form of a rifle shot. Lewis shouted again, "OK, it's your funeral. You've got exactly two minutes to come out, or I'll let them burn you out."

Another shot as an answer.

Lefty then turned to Timmons and told him, "Spread your men out all around the house so they can't escape unseen. Then fill a wagon with loose straw, and I'll set it on fire and point it at the front door of the house."

While the wagon load of straw was burning, Lefty and Shawn used it for cover and pushed it toward the house.

Lewis then shouted, "Last chance, Bradshaw. Come out and surrender or be fried like an egg. It's your last chance, so do it now."

This answer was two shots.

They pushed the wagon to the porch then took cover behind the watering trough. The wood on the house was dry from not being painted in years, so it ignited readily. It wasn't long before the entire front of the small house was engulfed. The sound of shooting had been replaced by choking and coughing.

Then Lewis yelled, "Come out and live, or stay there and die."

No response.

One of the crooked deputies tried to climb to safety through a side window, but was shot and killed by two of the night riders.

Then Sheriff Bradshaw emerged through the front door, a pistol in each hand, firing wildly. Lewis killed him instantly. The remaining deputy then emerged, holding a white flag. Lewis and Shawn let him pass, but he was killed by one of the vigilantes.

Then Timmons asked, "Should we try and put the fire out now?"

Lefty answered, "Hell, no! Let it burn. It is an evil house of an evil man, so it's good that they are all gone."

The Rangers led the three dead men, tied to their horses, rode back to town, and delivered them to the mayor.

Lewis then told him, "It was all done legal-like, so now you had better hire a new sheriff, and try to find an honest one this time."

The two Rangers found a boarding house, ate dinner, and

then went straight to bed so they could get an early start back to San Antonio the next morning. Another day of hard riding, and they arrived at the Ranger station a little after dark.

They were surprised to see Tall Paul and a group of Rangers still in the station so late.

Tall Paul greeted them, "Howdy boys. Everything go OK in Floresville?"

Shawn answered, "Yes, sir. We interrupted a group of vigilantes who had the sheriff trapped in his house. So we torched the house and killed the sheriff and his two crooked deputies."

"Good job. Now get a few hours of shut eye and be back here at dawn. The Austin Regiment is asking for us to help them set up an ambush for Sam Bass and his gang. For months now Bass has robbed banks and stagecoaches in the Dallas area. Now the Rangers there have a tip that he is headed for Austin, and we're going to set up ambushes on every road and trail into Austin and kill the thieving bastards. I have arranged to hire a special Wells Fargo stage coach pulled by six horses to take you to Austin. That will get you there a lot faster than horseback, and they will have horses there for you."

"Who all is going?" Lefty asked.

"You, Sweeney, O'Leary, Smith, Kline, and Ramsey. This is one job I would like to go along on, but I am needed here. Now get some sleep and be here at dawn," Evans told them.

They all hurried home and managed to get a few hours of sleep before heading back to the Ranger station the next morning. Shawn slept restlessly even though he was worn out from two days of hard riding and a gun battle. He didn't want to be late the next morning and miss the excitement in Austin.

Sam Bass was the most famous outlaw he had ever chased, and he was looking forward to it.

They all boarded the special coach. The ride was rough, the stage, cramped, but fast. They arrived in Austin by mid-afternoon. They were met by Major John B. Jones, the Ranger in charge of the Austin Frontier Regiment.

He broke up the San Antonio Rangers into groups of three and assigned an Austin Ranger to lead them. Lewis O'Leary and Sweeney were to be led by the famous Ranger John Armstrong. He was credited with the capture of John Wesley Hardin and his gang.

This group would guard the road from Round Rock, the one Major Jones guessed would be the one Bass was most likely to use.

The wait was longer than expected. Even though the Bass gang was being pursued by a group of Rangers led by Captain Junios Peek, they stopped long enough to rob the Williamson County bank and kill Sheriff Grimes in the process.

The long wait for the waiting Rangers was shortened by Armstrong's telling the story of how he captured John Wesley Hardin and his gang.

"Well, not very much to it. I chased that bastard and his gang all the way across Alabama and into Florida. At Pensacola I got on a train I heard they were on, and there they were. I drew my pistol and told them I was a Texas Ranger, and they were all under arrest. I hit Hardin hard over the head with my pistol and knocked him out.

"I got into a gun fight with the three other ones, killed one, and wounded another one, then the other one surrendered. Then I marched them over to the sheriff's office and had them locked up. Then I wired Captain McNelly, and he sent a prison wagon to get them. I was at Hardin's trial, and he was sentenced to 25 years in prison. That's all there was to it."

"Were you wounded?" Lefty asked.

"Nope. Just got a hole in my hat," he answered.

Then Armstrong shushed them, "They are coming our way. Get ready. Use your rifles at first, then switch to your pistols and kill every one of them. If any of them break through, all of you shoot at him. Under no circumstances can we let any of them get through the ambush."

They all gave a nod of understanding. When the gang rode closer, they saw there were eight of them.

Armstrong whispered, "When I start shooting, everyone else start shooting, too."

In less than five minutes Armstrong began shooting, and so did the other three Rangers. The first two outlaws fell and the other six returned fire and wheeled their horses about and attempted to retreat, but the volley of shots from the Rangers downed five of them. The last one was getting away, but Armstrong killed his horse. The rider, though wounded, was able to crawl away from the horse and into a field of standing corn. Armstrong checked the faces of the dead men, and then announced, "None of these men is Bass. Spread out and find him in that cornfield, but be careful. He is wounded and will kill you if he gets half a chance."

The sound of the gunfire brought the other Rangers from their positions.

Armstrong told them, "Go help the other men find Bass. He is wounded and hiding in that cornfield."

They instantly responded, and with pistols drawn they

entered the cornfield. Then the sound of O'Leary's voice broke the tension, "Here he is. He's still alive." They rushed to the sound of O'Leary's voice and found Bass, alive, but bleeding profusely from a stomach wound. He would die two hours later before they got him to the Ranger station.

Back at the station, Major Jones thanked the San Antonio Rangers, and they boarded the waiting special stagecoach for the trip back to San Antonio.

Upon arrival there Paul Evans told all of them, "Good work, men. Now take a few days off and get some rest."

# CHAPTER 20

## JOSEPH BEGINS THE BIGGEST CHALLENGE OF HIS LIFETIME

Patrick had spent time with Joseph telling him about rules, Charles Goodnight, the horses, the cattle, and how to behave around the chuck wagon.

The time for the cattle drive to begin was nearing, so Joseph left for Goodnight's ranch.

After hugs from his mother and handshakes from J.B. Rich and his brothers, he rode off. Patrick had drawn him a crude map, and he followed it to the ranch.

He was met by Goodnight and was introduced to Oliver Loving, the other owner of the cattle they would be driving.

He also met some of the other men he would be working with on the drive:

Mexican Bob—a tall skinny Mexican boy who would be his co-wrangler and would become his best friend on the drive.

Drago—A mysterious cowboy, who only used one name. He was a middle-aged man, with a graying half beard and full mustache, hiding part of his weather-beaten face. He never said where he was from, talked about his past, or discussed his family. Some of the hands said he was hiding from the law, but had no proof of that.

Crumbie—he was the new cook, replacing Cookie, who was too old to go on cattle drives anymore and now cooked for the ranch hands left behind.

Ears Amell—the young boy who was the new cook's helper. He was rightfully called Ears because of his big ears, which protruded from his boyish face.

Black Bill—a very dark-skinned black man, he had been a slave, a buffalo soldier belonging to a black Union regiment fighting Indians. They were called buffalo soldiers by their Indian enemies, who thought their kinky hair was like the hair on a buffalo.

Apache Jack—he was a half-breed. His mother was a white captive of the Apaches and his father was Golden Bear, sub-chief of the Mescalero Apaches.

Slick Willy—he earned his nickname by his abilities with a deck of cards, or a Colt pistol.

Mack McGuire—an affable red-headed, but balding Irishman, commonly called Mack the Knife. He earned his nickname demonstrating his skill with his bowie knife. He could carve figures with great attention to detail, cut down a small sapling, or throw the knife with deadly accuracy.

That evening Cookie cooked dinner for all of them, telling anyone who was willing to listen, "Sure wish I was goin' with you fellers, but my health just won't let me."

After dinner, Goodnight told Joseph, "From now on your name is Joe. Joseph sounds like a kid, and you ain't a kid no more."

"Yes, sir," Joseph answered.

The entire crew was in bed early, knowing the next morning they would be leaving on a journey of over 1,000 miles and working hard every day.

After an early breakfast the next morning, they saw the caravan all lined up ready to go.

First came the chuck wagon, followed by the supply wagon, then the water wagon, filled with barrels of water. This was followed by the wagon of gunnysacks for saving calves born on the trail. This would be followed by the 3,000 head of cattle, 200 head of horses for a breeding operation in Montana, and a string of 30 horses Joe and Mexican Bob would be wrangling, to be used as replacement horses during the drive.

Then with the 30 drovers, two wranglers, and two cooks assembled in a line, Goodnight and Loving stood on a wagon and told the group, "Oliver and I have studied the maps carefully and made a decision about which route to take to reach Montana. The western route is slightly shorter, but we would have mountains to cross. The eastern route will take us through the Indian nation, Kansas, Nebraska, and South Dakota into Montana.

"We have decided on the eastern route, where we will have flatter land to travel over, but a greater danger of Indian attacks. Now let's get going. We have a long way to travel."

As they traveled, it was apparent that Goodnight would be the trail boss and Loving would act as ramrod. All major decisions were to be made by Goodnight. The two men, although the best of friends, were completely different in manner. Goodnight was aloof and quiet, while Loving was more open and often joked around with the men.

Their plan was to travel 40 miles every day. At first with the livestock and drovers rested, they made the 40 miles easily. After several weeks, the distance traveled dwindled to 35 or even 30 miles a day.

After three weeks they were still in the Indian nation, and both Goodnight and Loving urged the men to keep up a faster pace. In six months the weather would worsen and slow their process considerably.

By the time they were well into Kansas, almost two months had passed.

Every day the routine was the same: up before dawn, get a quick breakfast of bacon and biscuits (sometimes with eggs), then have the cattle moving north as soon as the sun was up. At night the routine for Joe and Mexican Bob was always the same: string a static line of rope between two trees and tether all of the horses to it. This had to be done, and the horses fed, before the wranglers were allowed to eat. After they were in Kansas, Goodnight ordered the night hawks (night guards) doubled. He heard the Shawnee Indians were fighting with the army, and they didn't want the herd caught in the middle of any battles.

Also in Kansas they opted to hold up the herd for one day while Goodnight and Crumbie took the supply wagon into town to replenish their supplies.

While the herd was delayed, Loving became concerned when Black Bill had not returned from his scouting mission. He took Drago with him and went to search the trail ahead for some sign of Bill. They found him in agony with one arrow in his leg and another one in his shoulder. Beside him laid a dead Shawnee, scalping knife in his hand.

"What happened, Bill?" Oliver asked him.

"Three of those bastards ambushed me and got me good. I played dead, and that son of a whore came back to scalp me, and I shot him," Bill explained.

Oliver was able to pull out the arrow from Bill's shoulder easily, but the arrow in his leg was barbed and would not pull out. Bill told Drago, "Go ahead and push it through, but cut off the fletch first."

Drago took out his pocketknife, cut off the feather fletch, and shortened the arrow considerably. Then he used the butt of his pistol to push the arrow through, as Bill screamed in agony. Now with both arrows removed, Drago wrapped kerchiefs around the wounds and with Oliver's help was able to get Bill into his saddle. Then they rode slowly back to camp. Bill groaned with every step of the horse, but they soon had him safely in camp. All of the hands gathered around asking questions. Apache Jack walked to a nearby stream and returned with a handful of mud, which he applied to each of the wounds. The mud seemed to have a soothing effect, as Bill relaxed a bit after it was applied.

Oliver asked, "What did you put on his leg?"

"Creek mud. It's an old Indian remedy, and it keeps infection from setting in," Jack explained.

When Goodnight returned, Oliver told him of the happenings in his absence. Goodnight said, "Load him in the wagon with the gunny sacks; it will be easier on him than sitting on a horse. Now who will be our scout?"

"I will," Drago answered.

"OK then, leave right after you eat breakfast. Ride ahead

and find us some water for a camp tomorrow night," Goodnight commanded.

"Will do," Drago answered.

As soon as Crumbie and Ears got the supplies unloaded, they started cooking beans and hog fat and biscuits for a late dinner.

The next morning after breakfast Drago rode out to scout ahead, and the drovers got the herd moving north.

About mid-morning Goodnight heard the drovers yelling, "Riders coming into the herd."

Not knowing if the riders were friends or enemies, the drovers continued to keep the herd moving, but stayed alert.

As they drew closer, Charles and Oliver rode out to meet them. It was a sheriff and two deputies.

"Howdy, Sheriff," Goodnight yelled.

"Are you the boss man?" the sheriff asked.

"I am Charles Goodnight, and this is Oliver Loving. We are co-owners of this herd."

"Well, I'm Sheriff Dan Dobbins, sheriff of Barnes County, and these are my deputies. We're out here checking all of the herds looking for a murderer."

"I doubt if we have any murderers here. We all started out in Texas three months ago," Goodnight told him.

"If you don't mind, I'd like to take a look at your men," Dobbins said.

"That'll be OK—just don't keep them from doing their job. Who is this man you're looking for?" Goodnight asked.

"His name is Jim Johnson, and he shot and killed the man he caught in bed with his wife," Dobbins said.

"Where I come from, that's not murder," Goodnight remarked.

The sheriff explained, "To most folks it would not be murder, but in Barnesville it is. You see he killed Billy Bob Barnes, whose granddaddy founded the town, and his daddy is the mayor. I'm only looking for him because I want to keep my job. I don't blame him for killing Billy Bob. I might have done the same thing," Dobbins answered.

"What does he look like?" Oliver asked.

"He's middle-aged with graying hair, about 50 years old and a stocky build," Dobbins said.

Oliver and Charles looked at each other but said nothing. The sheriff just described Drago to a tee. Fortunately Drago was on a scouting trip.

Goodnight told the sheriff, "Sure, go ahead and look at all of the hands, but we don't have anyone here that looks like that."

Then Charles turned to Joe and winked as he told him, "Joe, you go and scout ahead and find us some water and graze. If you can't find it don't come back until dark."

Joe understood and responded, "Yes, sir. I'll find some and be back."

Joe then galloped off to find Drago and keep him away from the camp until dark.

After two hours of riding, he found Drago filling his canteen from a stream. He yelled, "Hey, Drago! It's me, Joe. Mr. Goodnight sent me to find you and tell you not to come back to the herd until dark."

"What's up?" Drago asked.

"Well, some sheriff from Barnesville is there with deputies looking for you," Joe explained.

"Oh, shit. Is Goodnight going to hand me over?" Drago asked.

"I don't think so. That's why he sent me out here to warn you," Joe said.

Then the two of them slowly rode back to the herd, timing their ride to arrive after dark.

When they neared the herd Drago yelled, "Attention in camp. Joe and Drago coming in."

Joe went to help tend the horses, while Drago went straight to see Goodnight.

"I hope I didn't cause any trouble today, boss. Are you going to fire me?" he meekly asked.

"Hell, no. I'm not going to fire you. As far as I'm concerned, you didn't do anything wrong. You know, when the sheriff finished looking over all the other men, I told him I hoped he never found you. Then he told me he hopes he never finds you, either. He is only trying to keep his job," Goodnight responded.

"Thanks, boss. I appreciate you looking out for me," Drago said.

Goodnight responded, "No thanks needed. Just do a good job and we'll all be fine. Now go get some chuck and turn in. By the way, find my water and graze?"

"Yes, sir. About 20 miles ahead is a good stand of high grass, and there is a creek about a mile further up the trail," Drago responded.

There were no surprises the next three weeks, only routine and boredom. The boredom was rudely interrupted one night by a sudden and violent thunderstorm. The night hawks were having their hands full trying to keep the cattle from stampeding by the noise of the thunder and wild bolts of lightning flashes. The rest of the crew threw on their slickers, saddled their mounts, and rode to help the night crew.

Goodnight was right in the center of the activity, shouting, "Keep the cattle out of those low areas. This is going to be a real gulley washer. Don't let any of those cattle bolt and stampede the others."

Crumbie and Ears Amell were also busy erecting a tarp and building a fire to cook coffee and prepare breakfast. They knew the hands would be tired and hungry after the cattle were brought under control.

In an hour or so the thunder and lightning subsided, but the rain continued for two days. Everything was flooded, and the ground was a muddy mess.

Crumbie and Ears did a good job keeping the hands' stomachs filled, but the herd was getting restless after the grass had been grazed out.

Loving and Goodnight met and decided to move the herd the second day to find fresh graze for them. Crumbie and Ears had a tough time digging the chuck wagon out of the mud. They had no luck trying to push it out, so Loving and Goodnight tied ropes to the wagon, tied them to their saddle horns, and pulled the wagon free of the muddy ruts. They traveled only 20 miles that day in the rain, but finally found a meadow full of good grass and bedded down the animals. They awoke the next morning to bright sunshine, lifting the spirits of the men and the animals.

For several more weeks they pressed the herd forward.

One morning at breakfast Goodnight announced, "Congratulations, men. We are about to cross the Platte River, and that means we're halfway and we did it in just five months, way ahead of schedule."

All of the hands cheered.

Then Loving added, "But the worst part of the journey lies ahead of us. From now on we'll probably have snow instead of rain, and we're likely to face the Sioux Indians instead of the Lakotas. So let's all keep our eyes peeled for hostiles."

The herd moved northward for another three weeks. They encountered only one light snowfall, which slowed their progress only slightly. Up until then they had only encountered a few Sioux hunting parties, who meant them no harm.

One afternoon Drago returned from his daily scouting trip at a full gallop. He reported to Goodnight, "There is a large band of Indians directly ahead. I think they are Sioux. It looks like they are forming a line completely across our path, trying to keep us from passing."

"Hell's fire," Goodnight remarked, and he took out his spyglass and tried to find the Indians. But a small hill ahead blocked his view. Loving overheard the conversation and rode out to tell the drovers, "Bunch up the herd, but don't let them stop. Indians ahead."

The hands herded the cattle closer together, but kept them moving forward. A half hour passed and Goodnight, still looking ahead with his spyglass, saw the hill ahead completely lined with Sioux warriors. He estimated there were over a hundred of them.

Then he said to Loving, "And you can bet there are a lot

more of them flanking us, and will completely surround us if we stop."

He handed the spyglass to Loving, who scanned the group of Indians ahead and told Goodnight, "They're not heavily armed. A few of them have muzzle-loading rifles, but the bulk of them have only bows and arrows, and some of them have only lances."

"What do you think we ought to do?"

"I think we should stampede the herd right into them. Let's see if their lances and bows and arrows are any match for the horns on our longhorn steers. I would much rather spend two days having to reassemble the herd than I would digging graves and burying my men. Do you agree?"

"I sure as hell do. I'll go tell the crew what we are going to do and tell them to have their guns ready," Loving said. And he rode off to talk to the men.

As the herd drew closer to the hill full of Indians, they stood fast. Then Goodnight started shooting, and the drovers also shot and whacked the steers on the rumps with their ropes, and the herd began moving forward. At first they moved slowly, but after more shooting and prodding by the cowboys, they were at a full stampede up the hill. The Sioux began to scatter. Some were not fast enough and were trampled. Then the drovers charged at a full gallop, shooting as they rode. The Indians began shooting back, but were in total confusion.

Goodnight remarked later that he doubted these Indians had ever seen anything like a stampeding herd of longhorns before. When it was all over the Sioux had completely scattered, but so had the herd. There were a few isolated gunfights between drovers and Indians, but the cowboys' superior weapons won most of them.

That night the guards were alert, and the rest of the men slept restlessly. There were no further signs of the Sioux that night.

The next day Goodnight and Loving began to count dead bodies. There were nine dead drovers. Poor unlucky Black Bill was one of them. He had just recovered from his previous wounds, only to be killed by a Sioux lance. They also counted thirty-five dead Sioux.

Three of the crew were slightly wounded, but without disabling wounds that would keep them from doing their jobs.

Also among the dead was Mexican Bob. This would force Joe to do double duty handling the horses, but he could manage it.

The drovers dug graves and buried their friends. Goodnight said to them, "Just leave the Sioux where they are. The other ones will come fetch them after we clear out of the area."

Then everyone turned to the difficult task of reforming the cattle into a moveable herd.

By the end of the second day, Goodnight and Loving came up with a rough count of the cattle and horses. They estimated they had lost 100 head of cattle, ten horses from the breeding stock, and seven horses from the spare riding horses. They considered themselves lucky the losses were not higher, considering what they had been through.

The herd was assembled, and Goodnight yelled the command, "Move 'em out," and the herd continued northward.

Drago prepared to leave to scout the trail ahead. Loving

told Goodnight, "I think I will go with Drago today. If there are any Sioux up ahead, two of us would have a better chance than one man alone."

Drago and Loving rode off. Just to feel a little safer, Loving tucked his 50 caliber Sharps Carbine into the scabbard on his saddle.

They rode about 15 miles from the herd when they saw a band of Sioux directly in their path. They both looked around for some sort of shelter, but there was none. They immediately started to retreat toward the safety of the herd.

The band of Indians was closing on them fast. Loving told Drago, "Stop here and we'll kill our horses and use them for shelter."

They shot the horses, laid down behind them, and prepared for the attack they knew was coming.

Drago with his Winchester and Loving with his Sharps started shooting at the attacking Sioux. The Indians were unaware of the range or accuracy of the Sharps, and Loving was able to kill four of them before they held up. Drago fired several times but only killed one of them. His Winchester was not nearly as effective as the Sharps at long range.

The odds were now reduced to 20 to two, but the pair was still in grave danger.

After a few minutes of discussion among themselves, the Sioux devised a new plan of attack.

They split into two groups and rode in two single file lines with several horse lengths between each rider. The plan was very effective. They managed to fire one arrow into Drago's left shoulder and two arrows into Loving's right leg, and one arrow into his left leg. The two white men were also able to inflict heavy casualties on the Sioux, killing five of them.

The Sioux fell back to a place out of rifle range and started planning another attack. Loving was in intense pain, even though Drago was able to pull out all three of the arrows from his legs. Likewise, Loving removed the arrow from Drago's shoulder.

Drago asked, "Boss, do you think you can walk?"

"I don't think so, at least not very far," Loving replied.

"What do you think we should do?" Drago asked.

"Well, if they don't attack us again soon, it will be dark, and if they're coming they'll wait until daylight. I think you should sneak out of here as soon as it's dark and make your way back to the herd and bring me some help," Loving told him.

"I'll try, boss, but it'll take me two days afoot to get there. I'll leave at dark, and leave you my Winchester, and get back as soon as I can," Drago explained.

"You're a good man, Drago. Just bring me some help, no matter how long it takes," Loving told him.

Drago shook Loving's hand, telling him, "Be back soon as I can," and he took off in a half run, taking only his pistol and a canteen of water.

Drago walked all night and half of the next day and still had not reached the herd. He had to stop and rest, but after one hour he set out again, and he was able to stumble into the camp, completely exhausted.

Goodnight questioned him, "What happened, and where is Oliver?"

After Drago explained, Goodnight told him, "Get something

to eat, and then sleep. You, me, and four riders are leaving at dawn to go get Oliver."

With a spare horse for Oliver, the six men rode in the direction Drago led them in. By mid-afternoon they reached Loving. He was alive, but in severe pain.

"Glad to see you men. I was afraid I was going to die in this God-forsaken place," Oliver told them.

"Did the redskins come back?" Drago asked him.

"No, if they had, a couple of them would be lying here beside me," Loving replied.

It took four of them, but they managed to get Loving onto a horse. They then followed the river to the west and before dark, arrived in Rapid City. They found a doctor and Drago and Goodnight carried Loving up the stairs into the doctor's office. Dr. Winans came out of the back to examine Oliver. After cutting away the jeans from both legs, his first remark was, "Tsk, tsk. Those are some nasty wounds. When did you receive them?"

"Three days ago," Loving answered.

"No wonder they are so infected," the doctor commented.

Then he looked at the wound in Drago's shoulder and said, "Your wound isn't infected at all. You must have kept moving after you were wounded."

"Yes, sir. I had to. I had to walk 15 miles back to the herd to get help for Mr. Loving," Drago answered.

"Well, by doing that you probably saved your own life. You kept the blood pumping, and the bleeding flushed out your wound," Dr. Winans told him.

The doctor bandaged his shoulder and then told him,

"I'm going to treat your friend's wounds now and give him something to make him sleep the night.

"All of you go check into the hotel down the street and come back here in the morning, and I'll know by then if I can save your friend's legs."

They all wished Oliver good luck, then left to find lodging. They also found a saloon and had a beer with a free sandwich.

They all slept well in comfortable beds, a treat from how they were used to sleeping.

At breakfast Goodnight told the others, "You men wait here, and I'll go see the doctor and come back and get you."

Goodnight hurried to the doctor's office, anxious to see how his old friend was doing.

Oliver was awake but still in pain as he greeted Goodnight, "Morning, Charles. The doctor has some bad news for me, and I'm glad you will be here to hear it with me. He said he wouldn't tell me until I had a friend here with me."

As soon as Dr. Winans came into the room, Goodnight asked him, "How is he, Doc?"

"Not very well. I wanted you here when he found out, but I'm going to have to cut off both legs to save his life," the doctor said solemnly.

"Like hell you are," Loving said, trying to sit up to no avail.

"Well, if I don't, you will be dead in three days. They both are infected with gangrene, and it's spreading into other parts of your body. Simply speaking, either the legs go, or you die," Doctor Winans told him.

"Well then, I'll just die. I'll be damned if I am going to be hauled around on a platform the rest of my life," Oliver said.

Charles well knew this was Oliver's determined voice, and he meant every word he was saying.

The doctor then said, "Well, sir, then all I can do is keep you comfortable the short time you have left."

Oliver told Charles, "Go get a bottle of whiskey and get drunk with me."

Goodnight did go to get a bottle of whiskey, but stopped first to tell his men the bad news about Loving.

"Men, I have some terrible news about Loving. Oliver won't let the doctor cut off his two legs to save his life, so the doctor says he will only live for three days. There is nothing more any of us can do for him. I'm going to stay here with him for as long as he lasts. I need for you men to return to the herd and get it going north. Drago, you will be in charge, so keep the herd moving, and I'll catch up as soon as I can. Oliver would have liked to have seen the herd in Montana, so do it for him."

All of the hands were in shock, but still obeyed orders from the boss. They left and talked all the way to the herd about how it would not be the same without Oliver joking around with them. Joe saw tears in some of the tough cowboys' eyes. He knew he felt like crying himself, but held back so as to not shame himself.

As they rode toward the herd they spotted five steers with the trail brand of their herd. They roped two of them and led them along with the other three following behind. The herding instinct was still strong, even among strays. They caught up with the herd by sundown and gave the bad news to the other drovers. Ears Amell broke into tears, Crumbie wept openly, and even Mack the Knife had tears in his eyes. All of the men united, though, and worked hard together under Drago's leadership. They were all determined to finish the drive and reach Montana.

Meanwhile, Goodnight took the whiskey and joined Oliver in downing several glasses of it as they had done together many times in the past.

Charles asked him, "Is there anything else I can do for you?"

"Yes, Charles. I want you to promise me you will take me back to Texas and bury me there. I don't want to lie forever in this damned foreign cold northern place. Do you promise?"

"Of course I promise. We have been good friends for too long for me not to do as you ask. Have I ever refused you anything?"

"No, you haven't, and I appreciate it. Just leave me here until you get the herd to Montana, then come back and get me, and haul my ass back home to Texas," Oliver said, his eyes welling with tears.

The doctor was wrong. Oliver didn't live three days; he died the second day, glad to be getting out of the pain he was suffering as the gangrene ate up all of his internal organs.

Doctor Winans remarked, "I'm sorry I couldn't do more for him, but he was a stubborn man and determined to do what he wanted to do."

That's OK. I thank you for what you did do for him. You're right; he was a stubborn man, but that's what made him so successful. Now is there an undertaker around I can get to look after him?" Charles asked.

"Yes. You stay here with your friend, and I'll go get O'Dell for you," Dr. Winans told him.

In a few minutes, Winans returned with a tall skinny man in a black suit, the undertaker.

Goodnight and O'Dell reached an agreement. O'Dell was to embalm Oliver, then flatten out some old grease buckets and make a metal box, then place Oliver in it and cover him with charcoal. He would then place the casket into a pine box. O'Dell was to keep the body until spring, when Charles would return for him.

O'Dell then said, "I'm sorry, but if you don't mind I would like payment in advance. I have had other men tell me they would return but never showed up."

Goodnight paid him, and then said, "When I tell you I will be back, I will."

"Yes, sir. I believe you will," O'Dell answered.

Goodnight paid the doctor. Then he went to the saloon, ordered two bourbons, clinked the glasses, drank them both, and said, "Good-bye, my old friend." Then he rode off to join the herd.

All of the crew ran to him asking questions about Loving and the future plans.

Goodnight told them all, "Nothing has changed except poor Loving won't be with us; we're still going to Montana. We'll set up a ranch, then next spring I'm going back to Rapid City to get Oliver and take him back to Texas for burial. I promised him I would do that, and that's what I'm going to do."

In two more months, despite going through a severe winter blizzard, they arrived in Montana. When the weather permitted, they spent the winter months building a log house, barn, and corral, and stringing barbed wire around the property.

During the coming months Goodnight and Crumbie made

several trips into Lewistown and bought food, hay, and oats to see them through the winter.

Everyone thought they might not make it through the winter, but when May arrived, the house, barn, and corral were finished. Most of the snow had melted.

Goodnight called a meeting and thanked all of them for their hard work. He paid them their wages plus a $200 bonus. He told them anyone who wanted to stay and man the ranch would have a job, as long as they wanted one. Anyone who wanted to leave could go, with his blessing. He told them he would be leaving the next morning to get Loving and take him to Texas, bury him, and then come back.

To a man, they agreed to stay on. Joe spoke with Goodnight later and told him, "Sir, if possible, I would like to go back with you. I miss my family and my girlfriend, and I'm kinda' homesick. You don't have to pay me."

"You've got a deal, my boy. I will be glad to have your company, and who knows if we'll run into any of our Sioux friends along the way. Here, take Oliver's old Sharps Carbine. It's yours now, and it might come in handy if there is trouble," Goodnight said.

The next morning they left in a wagon with supplies in the back and with two horses tethered behind. Good-byes were said, and they left. Their first stop was at the undertaking parlor in Rapid City. The undertaker and his helper loaded the pine box into the wagon, and Goodnight and Joe left for Texas.

Joe asked, "Won't the animals smell the flesh and attack the body?"

"Oh, hell no. He is in a tin box and covered with charcoal, so the animals won't get the scent," Goodnight explained.

They tried to stop mostly in towns where they could find a boarding house or hotel. Charles paid for all of it, even meals. In almost every town they passed through, people would ask him, "Are you Mr. Goodnight?" and "Is that your friend Mr. Loving in that box?"

Somehow the story had spread all over the territory.

They had traveled completely across South Dakota without seeing any signs of Indian activity, though they still remained on the alert. But they only saw Indian hunting parties and migrations.

They were now camping out, sleeping at night without a fire and eating cold beef jerky, instead of building a fire to cook.

Their third day in Nebraska they had a stroke of good luck when they ran into an army patrol, and they traveled with them to Fort Fremont. That night they had their first good, hot meal in three days, and their first restful sleep on straw in the stable.

The colonel in charge of the fort explained that the Indians were stirred up by all of the travelers on their way from the south and east. Gold had been discovered in the Black Hills, and they knew the government would break the treaty they made with them, in favor of the gold miners.

The next morning they left the fort and continued south. In three days they crossed into Indian Territory. It took them ten more days to arrive at trading post number one. Here they found a small hotel with a dining room, and more importantly for Joseph, a telegraph office. Joe lost no time in sending a wire to his mother and J.B. Rich, saying he expected to be home the following month. He had written many letters home during his travels but expected and got no replies, because he had no address where they could write him.

Their next stop was in trading post number two, only three weeks' travel to Goodnight's ranch.

That evening as they ate at a small diner, they knew they were getting close to home because they ordered barbequed brisket, beans, and fried potatoes. They each ate two helpings. There was no hotel or boarding house, so they bedded down in a stable with the horses.

The rest of the way home they saw no Indians. They did see a few smoke signals going up, but nothing to follow up on these signs.

When they arrived at Goodnight's ranch, it was mid-afternoon. Cookie was the first to greet them, asking, "Where is Mr. Loving?"

Goodnight pointed to the box saying, "He's in there. The Sioux killed him in South Dakota. I promised him I would bury him in Texas, and that's what I am going to do tomorrow."

Joseph told Goodnight, "It's too late to start for home tonight; would it be OK if I spend the night in the bunk house, and leave first thing in the morning?"

"That will be fine, son, and tonight we'll enjoy one of Cookie's fine meals," Goodnight told him.

Early the next morning Joseph said his good-byes and left for home. It would be good to be home.

His horse had been well cared for, and Joseph was glad to be riding him again. Cookie had packed him ham sandwiches, and he ate them in the saddle so he could get home without stopping. It was mid-afternoon when he arrived at the boarding house.

# CHAPTER 21

# THE NOT-SO-HAPPY
# HOMECOMING FOR JOSEPH

Joseph tied his horse to the hitching post, took his bedroll and Sharps rifle, and rushed up the stairs to the apartment over the carriage house. He was surprised to see the entire family assembled in the parlor, except for their mother.

He was greeted warmly by his brothers and Pam, as well as Father Lynch.

"Where is Mama?" he asked.

Patrick said, "Come in here and sit down. We have some bad news to tell you."

Pam interrupted saying, "You boys go ahead and talk. I'm going to ride over and get Linda. She will be so glad you are home."

"Is Mama OK?" Joseph asked.

Patrick answered, "She is fine. She is at the hospital with J.B. He has been shot but should be OK later on."

"Who in the hell shot him?" Joseph wanted to know.

Shawn answered him, "We really don't know yet. I'll let Mama tell you the whole story; she knows more than the rest of us."

Father Lynch then offered, "I went to see him last night. I spoke with the doctor, and he told me J.B. is out of danger, and probably could go home in two days if we hire a private duty nurse for him. He had four double-ought buck shot in his chest, but they missed his heart and lungs. They were able to remove them, but he has lost a lot of blood. I have been praying for him."

Then Patrick told Joseph, "Mama has hired Pinkerton guards for him in case whoever did it tries to finish the job."

Then Joseph asked, "What the hell do we need Pinkerton guards for? We can do it ourselves."

Patrick said, "Sure, we can do that when we get him home in his own bed."

Their talk was interrupted as Linda rushed into the room. She ran directly to Joseph, kissed him, and held him close. They were wrapped around each other like two snakes ready to mate.

Patrick warned them, "Careful kids! Father Lynch is here, and you don't want to offend him."

"That's OK, Patrick. There is nothing they are doing that would offend me…or God. We both understand they are two young people in love and have been separated for a long time," Lynch said.

Patricia rushed herself in the kitchen and returned with a huge tureen of potato soup and cheese sandwiches and said, "Sorry folks, but this is the best I could do on short notice."

Everyone ate their fill. After eating, Father Lynch left for home, and the brothers broke out a bottle of Irish whiskey. They were joined by Pam and Linda as they toasted Joseph's safe return and wished J.B. a speedy recovery.

Later Joseph drove Linda home. As they drove along he told her, "I hope it won't be too long until I don't have to take you home at night."

"I would stay with you tonight, if it wouldn't shame us with the others," Linda answered.

"Just as soon as we get this mess with J.B. cleared up, I would like for us to be married, if that's OK with you," Joseph told her.

"Of course, that's fine with me. I hope how soon," she replied.

They sat in the buggy together talking and kissing until Shawn rode up with Pam. Then the girls went into their home and the boys drove home. Early the next morning the four brothers went to J.B.'s house to see their mother.

She greeted Joseph warmly first, because he had been away for two years, but she had hugs and kisses enough for the other three boys, too.

As they all sat talking, Patrick said, "Mama, tell us what J.B. said happened to him."

"Well, J.B. told me about three months ago they wanted to expand and overhaul the Dallas Palace, so the three partners all voted to bring in two more partners to get some new money into the casino. He said they were Bradley Stine, who had made his fortune in a machine shop making oil well equipment for the booming oil business, and Harry Traugh was the other one. He made a lot of money in drilling oil wells. Soon after they took a place on the board, they began lobbying for the addition of a brothel to the casino.

"Every time they brought it up, they were overruled by the original board members, J.B., Jim Stock, and Ben Dooley.

"That started the feud, and J.B. thinks the two new board members arranged to have him and Dooley killed so they could have their way and prevail on the board, because with J.B. and Ben dead they would be the majority on the board," Anna told them.

"Those dirty bastards," Patrick uttered.

He expected a rebuke from Anna for saying that, but Anna agreed saying, "That's what they are, and worse, trying to kill my J.B. just to build a whore house."

After this discussion, they all went to the hospital to see J.B. and maybe hear some more of the story.

The two Pinkerton guards gave instant access to the room for Anna, and seeing the Ranger badge on Shawn, they also waved him to enter. Before the other boys would be admitted, Anna had to explain they were also her sons.

J.B.'s eyes brightened when he saw all of them come into the room. He also saw Joseph and gave him a broad smile and said, "Well, Joseph, I see Charles got you home safely. How is the old horse thief anyway?"

Patrick answered, "He is fine, but Mr. Loving was killed by Indians in South Dakota."

"That's too bad. Oliver was a good man," J.B. responded.

Anna kissed her husband and asked, "How do you feel? Do you think you might be up to going home tomorrow afternoon?"

"I'll do that if I have to crawl. And let me say, I have been doing a lot of thinking. Patrick, I would like you to temporarily take my place on the board at the Palace. That will keep those bushwhackers Stine and Traugh from having a majority and going ahead with their evil plans. Will you do it?"

"I'd be honored, sir, but only until you are up to going back," Patrick replied.

"Fine, fine, I'll have the papers drawn up tomorrow," J.B. answered.

Then Shawn interrupted, "Now, sir, tell us what happened."

"Well, Ben and I were taking a large deposit to the bank after a very profitable weekend. I was driving the buggy and Ben was holding the cash when we noticed two men blocking the road ahead of us. One was a Mexican holding a double-barreled shotgun, and the other one had his pistol drawn.

"At first I thought it was a hold up, but then I remembered no one except our partners knew what we were doing, and we were always careful to change our route every week. I drew my pistol, and when the Mexican saw me, he shot me with the shotgun. Luckily, he was far enough away I missed the worst of the blast, but the white man shot and killed poor Ben. I was still conscious and watched them run away, not even bothering to take the bank deposit. And, oh yes, the white man had a black patch over his right eye and an anchor tattoo on his left arm," Rich related.

"But how did you get here?" Shawn asked.

"Well, thank God, a Good Samaritan heard the shooting, ran to us, and drove us both here," J.B. answered.

Then Shawn asked, "What do you intend to do now?"

"I don't intend to do anything. I am going to track down the sons of bitches who shot us, connect them with our new greedy partners, and have the whole bunch of them locked up," J.B. said.

"Have you talked to the sheriff?" Shawn asked.

"I certainly did, but it was like talking to a brick wall. I have heard rumors Sheriff Gage is not on the up and up, and I'm starting to believe the rumors may be true," J.B. told him.

Then Shawn volunteered, "I'll go see police Chief Baker tomorrow and see what he thinks. I know he is a good friend of my boss, Paul Evans, so he must be honest."

Anna cut the talking short when she said, "I think we had all better get out of here now and let J.B. rest so we can take him home tomorrow." They all left.

The next morning Shawn and Patrick went to see Chief Bill Baker at the Dallas Police station.

They introduced themselves, and seeing the Ranger badge on Shawn, he became very interested. "I know who you boys are. How is J.B. doing?" Baker asked.

"Looks like he is going to make it. We're hoping to take him home this afternoon," Patrick told him.

"That's good news, but what can I do for you?" Baker asked.

Shawn replied, "I wonder if you can tell us about the shooting?"

"I'm sorry, but I can't help you. The Dallas Palace is in the county, and the shooting also took place in Tarrant County, so I have no jurisdiction there. That is Sheriff Gage's jurisdiction, and he is very jealous of his territory," Chief Baker told them.

"Yes, sir, we understand that, but we have heard rumors that Sheriff Gage is not completely honest," Shawn told him.

Baker replied, "I don't deal in rumors. Shawn, you should know Texas Rangers handle all of those complaints. You are a Ranger, so go over to the Ranger station in Garland and talk to them."

The boys thanked Chief Gage and left. On the way out Patrick told Shawn, "Well, he isn't going to be any help at all."

"I agree. Tomorrow I will go see the Rangers in Garland, but today let's get J.B. home," Shawn answered.

That afternoon Anna and Patricia went in a buggy, Shawn and Patrick followed in another buggy, and Mark and Joseph followed in a wagon with a pallet in the wagon bed. All of the boys were heavily armed, fearing another attack on J.B.'s life might be attempted.

Anna went into the hospital, discharged the Pinkertons, and with the help of a nurse, wheeled J.B. out of the hospital and on the pallet in the wagon. A private nurse Anna hired followed them outside. The ride home was uneventful. Even so, all of them remained on the alert, just in case. When they reached J.B.'s home, Mark and Joseph helped J.B. get inside to the bed Anna had prepared for him in the parlor. She did not think he could manage to climb the steps to his regular bedroom. Anna and the nurse got J.B. into the bed, and the boys got busy setting up a schedule so that two of them would be on guard in the house at all times.

After J.B. was comfortable, everyone was introduced to the private duty nurse Anna had employed. She was introduced as Helen Hayes, a middle-aged lady, who had been a nurse for ten years. She explained she would come every morning, change his bandages, administer his medications, and do whatever else she was asked to do. Later that afternoon Patricia, Pam, and Linda arrived. They helped the cook, Cecelia, prepare a large dinner, and at five they all sat down for the first family dinner in years.

Anna said grace and thanked God for the food, for saving J.B., and for her four sons.

The next morning Joseph went with Shawn to the Ranger station in Garland. Shawn introduced himself and was immediately ushered in to see Captain Billy Darling, second in command of the Garland Frontier Regiment.

Hearing Shawn was from San Antonio, Darling asked, "How is that old horse thief, Tall Paul?"

"He is fine, sir, and this is my brother Joseph. He just got back from a two-year cattle drive to Montana."

Darling shook Joseph's hand and said, "Oh, you were with Goodnight. That's too bad about Loving. He was a good man."

Shawn thought, *Not much escapes this man.*

"What can I do for a fellow Ranger?" Darling asked.

"Well, sir, our stepfather, J.B. Rich, was shot and his partner Ben Dooley was killed," Shawn told him.

"Oh, yeah, I heard about that. It was an attempted robbery, wasn't it?" Darling answered.

"No, sir. J.B. thinks it was an attempt to kill him and his partner, so two of his other partners could get control of the Dallas Palace and add a whore house to the complex," Shawn said.

"Those are pretty serious charges. Did J.B. tell Sheriff Gage about his suspicions?" Darling asked.

"He said he did try, but the sheriff wasn't too interested. J.B. said he heard rumors Sheriff Gage wasn't completely honest," Shawn told him.

"Well, I'm sorry, but I can't act on rumors. Bring me some proof and I'll stomp on Gage like he's a bug," Darling told them.

Feeling they were getting nowhere, Shawn and Joseph told Darling they would try and get proof and they left. When they got home they met with Mark and Patrick and told them they had gotten nowhere with the police chief or the Rangers.

Patrick was on the verge of rage, his face turning red, when he said, "OK, damn it to hell. If they want proof, we'll get some for them. Friday is the next scheduled Palace board meeting, and I'm going to attend it and present them with J.B.'s documents and take my seat on the board."

With all of the excitement that had happened since he got home, Shawn had not had a chance to ask about Conchita. Now he did inquire about her with Patricia, who told him her mother died in Mexico and that Conchita went there for the funeral. She would be back next week.

Shawn had only used up half of his thirty days of leave, so he would still be home when Conchita got back. He had never gotten around to hiring a housekeeper for his house in San Antonio, and he was toying with the idea of offering the job to Conchita. After all, he had never found out if Tih's claim was true. Did they, or didn't they? The answer eluded him. He had to know.

J.B. continued to improve steadily. He was now able to sit up and take his meals, and thanks to nurse Hayes he was out of pain and had no infection.

The next Friday morning Patrick left to attend his first board meeting at the Dallas Palace.

He took Shawn with him, in case there was trouble. Mark and Joseph remained at home to guard J.B.

As they walked into the Palace, they were met by Jim Stock, one of the original board members. Stock recognized them from the bachelor party and took them aside to talk to them.

He said, "J.B. told me what he was going to do, and I'm so relieved. Stine and Traugh have me outvoted two to one, and I was afraid they would ram something through before J.B. got back."

Patrick responded, "Well, that ain't going to happen. If you and I stick together, we can block everything until J.B. gets back."

"Fine. Let's go have the meeting," Stock responded.

"I'll wait in the bar, but if I hear any commotion, I'll come running," Shawn told them.

At the bar, Shawn sipped a beer and introduced himself to Amos, the bartender. Amos was a large black man with a huge smile and a friendly face.

Amos confided in Shawn, "I sure hope they don't turn this

place into a whore house. If they do, I'll have to quit. I like it here the way it is."

"That ain't gonna happen. My brother Patrick is going to take J.B.'s place on the board, and he won't allow that to happen," Shawn reassured him.

"Well, thank the good Lord for that," Amos said.

Upstairs the meeting of the board was taking place. Stine and Traugh were disappointed that Patrick would be taking J.B.'s place on the board, but grudgingly accepted the papers J.B.'s attorney had prepared.

The board was deadlocked with a vote of two to two on every issue brought up, so they adjourned the meeting early.

Patrick saw he was not going to get anywhere using tact and niceness, so he decided to switch tactics and try accusations and threats. As they all got up to leave the table, he looked at Traugh and Stine and told them, "I hate to accuse you two, but J.B. thinks you hired someone to kill him and Dooley, and I believe that too."

"If you think that, why don't you go see Sheriff Gage?" Stine said.

"J.B. tried that but got no cooperation. I have another approach I can take. My brother is a Texas Ranger, and he is waiting for me in the bar. We'll see what he can uncover," Patrick told them.

Stine and Traugh stormed out of the room. Patrick warned Jim Stock, "Jim, you had better watch your back. Those two conniving bastards would do anything to gain control of this place."

"I have been ever since the shooting, and I will certainly continue," Stock said.

Then Stock and Patrick met Shawn in the bar, and moved to a table where they could talk in private.

Shawn told them, "I befriended Amos, the bartender, and he told me in confidence that he saw Stine and a one-eyed man talking quietly at a corner table a couple of weeks ago."

"I knew it. Now we have to locate the one-eyed man and the Mexican, and we can make them tell who hired them. Then we can hang the whole bunch of them," Patrick said.

That afternoon Shawn went to the office of Sheriff Gage and asked permission to look through his wanted posters. There were plenty of posters of Mexicans, but he could not find one of a one-eyed man.

Sheriff Gage said to him, "I know you are a Texas Ranger, but why are you interested in my wanted posters?"

"Yes, sir, I am a Texas Ranger, but I am also a stepson of J.B. Rich, and I am looking for the bastards who shot him," Shawn explained.

Sheriff Gage's face paled but he tried to recover by saying, "Well, be sure and let me know if I can be of help." Shawn thanked him and left.

Patricia spent the morning checking on the boarding house, then picked up Pam and Linda and returned to the Rich's house to help Anna prepare dinner for everyone.

J.B. was feeling well enough to join them at the table for dinner. Patrick said the grace then told everyone, "We are going to have to be double cautious around here from now on. Shawn and I stirred up a hornet's nest today when we told Stine, Traugh, and the sheriff we were working to find the men that shot J.B. and Dooley and the people who hired them."

J.B. cautioned them, "You guys be very careful. You are

dealing with vicious men, and they stand to lose a lot of money if you are successful in gaining control of the Palace."

After dinner the boys were talking. Shawn told them he had not checked the wanted posters at the Ranger station, so the next morning he went there.

Darling met him and said, "I hope you are bringing me some proof. Since we talked the other day, I made some inquiries about Sheriff Gage and learned J.B. is probably right about him."

"No, sir. I don't have proof yet, but J.B. remembers the two who shot them. One was a Mexican, and the other was white with a patch over one eye and an anchor tattoo on his arm. If it is OK with you, I'd like to look through your wanted posters and see if I can find them," Shawn related.

"Sure. You go ahead, and if you see anyone let me know," Darling said.

CHAPTER 22

# THE NOOSE TIGHTENS
# AROUND THE CONSPIRATORS

Shawn spent an hour carefully going through the posters. Finally he found one who might fill the bill of one of the murderers.

Thrilled, he yelled out, "Captain Darling, I think I found one."

Darling rushed in, and the two of them examined the poster Shawn located. It read:

Wanted Dead or Alive:
Sailor Sam Stone. $1,000 reward. Wanted for
the murder of Captain Bill Fender, Skipper of
the steamboat Delta Queen. Use caution. He is
a vicious killer. Contact U.S. Marshal's office in
New Orleans, Louisiana Territory.

There was a crude drawing of a man, but it was impossible
to make out features. The black patch over his right eye was
clearly visible though. There was no mention of a tattoo.

Darling was also excited and told Shawn, "Good going. You
may have found a good starting place. I'll wire the Marshal's
office and see if I can find out anything more about him. Check
with me tomorrow."

Excited to share the news, Shawn rushed home to tell J.B.
and his brothers. He excitedly told the family of his findings.

Patrick told him, "That's good news, but we also might have
something. A sleazy-looking Mexican came to the door and
asked if he could give us a quote on doing our yard work. He
looked suspicious because his hands were not calloused as they
would have been if he did manual labor."

"Why didn't you grab him?" Shawn asked.

"Hell, we can't just grab every Mexican in town. J.B. was
sleeping, so I told him to come back in the morning when
J.B. is awake, and we'll see if J.B. can identify him. If he does
remember him, we'll grab him then," Patrick responded.

The next morning Captain Darling showed up with news.
After being introduced to the family, he sat down at the table
and had coffee with all of them.

He said, "I have some news. I got a return wire from the

Marshal's office in New Orleans. Sailor Stone does have an anchor tattoo on his left arm. I think he is the man we are looking for. He is last reported as being in Galveston, but he could easily have made his way here."

Then Patrick told Darling about the visit from the Mexican and that he was coming back there this morning.

"Let's hope he comes while I am here, and I'll arrest him," Darling announced.

They were on their fourth cup of coffee when they heard a horse approaching. Patrick looked out the window and started giving orders like he was the person in charge.

"You girls all get upstairs in case there is shooting. Mama, you put J.B. in a place where he can see but not be seen. Shawn, you and Captain Darling get out of sight. Your badges might scare him off," he commanded.

Mark and Joseph continued to sit at the table, their pistols concealed under napkins.

Patrick answered the door and admitted the Mexican, who said, *"Buenos dias, senor."*

"And good morning to you. Please come in and have a cup of coffee," Patrick told him.

Before they even reached the table, J.B. yelled from behind a curtain, "That's the son of a bitch. Get him."

The boys jumped the Mexican and took away his pistol and knife. Captain Darling and Shawn came out and Darling put manacles on him.

The Mexican's face showed a mixture of shock, surprise, and fear, as he asked, "What's this all about?"

"You're under arrest for the murder of Ben Dooley and the attempted murder of J.B. Rich," Darling told him.

"Me no do that," he lied.

J.B. answered, "Like hell you didn't. I remember you all too well. Now where is Sailor Stone?"

No answer from the Mexican. "What is your name?" Darling asked. *"Como se llama?"*

"Juan Ramos," came the answer in a weak voice.

Darling then asked him, "Where is Sailor Stone? And don't tell me you don't know. You might as well tell me now, or I'll take you back to the Ranger station. We have a special room there where I can work you over, and no one can hear you scream. Believe me, you will tell me."

All other emotions except fear vanished from his face as he said, "They're hiding the sailor in the wine cellar of the Dallas Palace. Sheriff Gage told them you were looking for him."

"I knew that son of a bitch Gage was crooked, but I sure didn't know he was in on this," J.B. angrily said.

Darling caught that slip about Sheriff Gage knowing about Sailor Stone's part in the murder. He thought to himself, *I have a leak in my office. That's the only way Gage could have known that we were on to Stone.*

"OK. I'm going to lock up this one. Then I'll take some Rangers and go to the Palace and get the rest of them," Darling said.

Shawn interrupted, "Excuse me, sir, but my brothers and I would like to go arrest them. Would that be OK?"

"Alright. I owe you that much, but don't do anything until I get back here with some other Rangers, and we can back you up," Darling told them.

Darling left to take the Mexican to lock up; the four brothers had a meeting.

J.B. interrupted them saying, "I sure wish I could go with you. Please be careful. These are dangerous, determined men with a lot to lose."

Anna added, "Please use caution. I don't want to lose another son."

While they waited, the brothers decided to all wear the blue blazers J.B. had given them.

By the time Darling returned with four other Rangers, the four brothers were all seated in the wagon. They all wore holstered pistols and were all armed with Winchesters, except Shawn. He was carrying the Sharps rifle Goodnight had given to Joseph.

Patrick drove the wagon to the Palace, with the five Rangers lagging back about a block.

When they arrived, they found Stine and Traugh seated in the otherwise empty bar.

The four brothers stormed in with Shawn yelling, "Put your weapons on the table, then get up slowly. If you don't you will find out what a big bore Sharps can do to a man at close range, and it is not a pretty sight."

Stine defiantly asked, "What the hell is the idea of this?"

Shawn answered, "I am Texas Ranger Shawn Sweeney, and you both are under arrest for conspiracy to commit murder. Traugh, you go down to the wine cellar and bring the sailor up here, unarmed, and with his hands high in the air. Makes me no never mind whether you do or not. I'd just as soon kill all of you right here and now."

Traugh laid down his pistol and went to the wine cellar to get Sailor Stone, but Stine hesitated.

Patrick told him, "Go ahead, Stine, go for it. I would like the pleasure of killing you myself, right here and now."

Stine's face paled but he obeyed, laid down his pistol, and put his hands over his head.

Mark and Joseph moved to opposite sides of the room so they could have Traugh and the sailor in a cross fire if they resisted. The boys were surprised, but Traugh and Stone emerged as meek as lambs with their hands over their heads.

Suddenly the five Rangers came into the room. Darling said to Sailor Stone, "Well, we got you. After we try you for murder and attempted murder, and conspiracy to commit murder, you will be in prison for a long time. Then the federal marshals in New Orleans will come and get you and take you back to New Orleans and hang you for the murder you did there."

Then Darling told the brothers, "Good work, men. My Rangers can take these three to the station and lock them up. I'm going to go arrest Sheriff Gage and lock him up and find out who his spy in my office is."

Then he got Shawn off to one side and told him, "Shawn, you are a fine Ranger, as soon as I find the Ranger who told Gage, I'm going to fire him, and I'll have an opening for you in my office. Want the job, if Paul Evans will cut you loose?"

"Yes, sir. I would like that. I would be closer to my family that way," Shawn said.

Unbeknownst to them all, Amos, the barkeeper, had been hiding and had seen the whole scenario. He told them, "Thank you for what you did. Please let me buy you all a drink on the house."

Shawn told him, "I think we can all use a short drink. Will you join us?"

"Thanks, but I don't drink a drop," Amos answered him.

When the brothers arrived back at the house, J.B. and the girls were greatly relieved they were all OK. Shawn had an additional surprise as Conchita was among the people awaiting their return. She rushed to Shawn.

He told her, "I was sorry to hear about your mother."

*"Gracias.* Now kiss me," she answered.

He did and held the kiss until he became self-conscious about his family watching. Then the boys spent a lot of time answering questions from J.B. and the girls. They downplayed the danger involved. Patrick told J.B., "You should give Amos, the bartender, a nice raise. He told Shawn about seeing Stine with Stone in the bar, and he probably will testify against Stine in the trial."

J.B. agreed, "I'll take care of that. Patrick, Jim Stock is coming over here in a little bit, and I'd like you to be present when I talk to him."

Patrick was puzzled but said he would be available.

When Stock arrived, J.B. ushered him into his office and Patrick followed. J.B. got right down to business.

"Jim, we are going to have to rebuild the board. Have anyone in mind?"

"Yes, sir—I have. George Lumley is a friend of mine, a damned good horse breeder, and has some money to invest. I spoke with him before, but he wasn't interested because he hated Stine. It seems Stine cheated him on a business deal once, and he didn't want to sit on the same board with him," Stock said.

"Sure, I know him. He is fine with me. Now I haven't asked

him yet, but I'd like to propose Patrick, here, after I ask him some questions."

"Patrick, if you sat on our board of directors, would you feel obligated to vote the way I do every time?" J.B. asked.

"No, sir, not if I thought you were wrong," Patrick answered.

"Do you think you could get along with me, Jim Stock, and this Lumley fellow?" J.B. asked.

"I don't know Mr. Lumley, but I know you and Mr. Stock, and I sure as hell can get along with you two," Patrick responded.

"Sound OK with you, Jim?" J.B. asked.

"Fine with me. Patrick and his brothers saved my neck once, and I have good reason to trust him," Stock responded.

"Good enough. We'll vote on them at the board meeting next month," J.B. stated.

Patrick was so happy he could hardly wait to tell Patricia, but he tried to conceal his feelings from J.B. and Stock. He was going to be a director of the Dallas Palace.

When he had the opportunity, he told Patricia, who told him, "Oh, Patrick, I am so proud of you. Your mother told me this was going to happen, but I could hardly believe it."

"Then Mama already knew?" Patrick said.

"Of course she did, but she wanted to let J.B. surprise you," Patricia told him.

That evening at dinner J.B. broke the news to all of the others. Patrick got congratulations from all of his brothers and their girlfriends. More good news was in store for the family later that evening when Captain Darling came by the house with good news for Shawn.

"Shawn, I had a return wire from Paul Evans. He hates to

lose you but has agreed to release you. He said you have earned it. So, effective next Monday you will be working for me."

"Thank you very much sir, but I'll have to go to San Antonio and pick up my things to move back here," Shawn told him.

"OK, take a couple of days to move your things, but don't take too long," Darling told him.

"Yes, sir. Did you find out who was feeding information to Sheriff Gage?" Shawn asked.

"Sure as hell did. It was Ranger Wooley, and I fired him on the spot. It turned out Gage was his uncle, so I guess he had reason to tell him. He is an arrogant little snot. He told me he will run for sheriff next time to replace his uncle, but I sure as hell won't vote for him," Darling stated.

Later, Shawn was driving Conchita home and he asked her, "Want to go to San Antonio and help me move?"

"Of course I do. When do we leave?" she asked.

"Day after tomorrow. I'll borrow Mama's wagon, and we can use it to move my stuff back," Shawn said.

Instead of answering, Conchita wrapped around him kissing and hugging him.

On Monday morning Shawn and Conchita were off for San Antonio, Shawn driving the team of horses, and Conchita sitting close to him, hugging and kissing him, and telling him how much she loved him.

They stopped in Georgetown to rest the horses and get lunch in a diner. When they were on the way again Shawn showed her the spot where they had the gun battle with the Sam Bass gang.

"Oh, Shawn, you have such a dangerous job. I worry about you so much," Conchita told him.

"Please don't worry about me. I am always careful not to get into a mess I can't get out of," he reassured her.

It was dark before they arrived at the house Shawn had rented. He took her in and showed her around before he went back outside to tend to the horses. When he walked back inside he found Conchita was already fixing sandwiches for them. He located a bottle of wine and poured them both a glass.

After the sandwiches were eaten and the bottle of wine emptied, they both suddenly felt very tired. The long trip from Dallas had tired them, the sandwiches had filled their stomachs, and the wine had numbed their minds, so they both took off their boots and lay down in bed, fully dressed.

Sometime during the night, Shawn woke up feeling cold. He had no idea of the time, but he knew he was cold. No wonder he felt cold; someone had removed his jeans, long johns, and socks, and he was naked from the waist down. As he began to cover himself with the blanket from the foot of the bed, he noticed Conchita lying beside him, completely naked, but with her head turned away from him. He covered them both with the blanket.

*Oh no, did it happen again, and I can't remember it this time either?*

He didn't know if they had done it or not. But he did know he was still tired and sleepy, and he fell off to sleep. When he awoke again, it must have been morning because he saw the sun peeking through a division in the shutter. Conchita was still beside him, but now was facing him, one arm around his chest. Having her close like this felt good to him.

For a few minutes he laid there, enjoying the moment, and

not wanting to disturb Conchita. Soon she stirred, then opened her eyes, and began kissing him.

Embarrassed, he asked Conchita, "What happened? Did we make love?"

She rubbed her eyes and replied, "No, you silly boy. If we had made love, believe me, you would remember. Here, let me show you what I mean."

Then she rolled over on top of him, began kissing him, and rubbing every part of his body she could reach. Then she took his left hand and guided it to her right breast then began gyrating the lower part of her body. Shawn reciprocated, and soon Shawn was issuing low grunts, and Conchita uttering screams of delight.

There was no doubt they had done it, and there was also no doubt that Shawn would remember it.

They remained in bed for several more minutes talking, kissing, and holding each other, until Shawn remembered he had to go see Tall Paul, then load his stuff into the wagon.

As Shawn dressed, Conchita put on her shirt and went into the kitchen and began making coffee. Was that the first time for you?" she asked.

"I wasn't sure if it was or not, but now I know it was the first time. A Cherokee girl in Oklahoma also woke up next to me and tried to make me believe we had done it, but now I know she lied to me," he explained.

"Well, I hate to say it wasn't the first time for me, but it was the best time. I hope you won't be mad at me, but I didn't want to lie to you," she told him.

"Of course I won't be mad at you. Our life together starts now, and the past is over and done with," he said.

"No wonder I love you so much. You are a wonderful, loving man, and I love you very much," she said and kissed him.

After she had cooked his breakfast, he told her, "You stay here and rest. I'm going to the Ranger station to tell them all good-bye, then I'll come back and load the wagon, and we can get an early start for home in the morning."

"Whatever you say, my love," she responded.

Shawn had a good visit at the Ranger station.

He told Tall Paul, "Thank you, sir, for releasing me to go to Garland. I have enjoyed my time here and the good friends I made here, but I really need to be closer to home. Mama isn't getting any younger, and I need to spend more time with her."

"I certainly understand that. You did a good job for me, and I know you will do a good job for Darling. Good luck to you. You will always be welcome here," Evans told him.

Shawn then told Lefty and his other friends good-bye and left for his house to load the wagon. On the way he bought another bottle of wine to share with Conchita for the evening.

She was fixing ham and eggs for supper to finish up the perishable foods they had left. She had also packed up all of the dishes, pots, and pans ready for loading. Then she helped Shawn to carry everything to the wagon. At dinner they started drinking the wine, and finished it before they went into the bedroom. Then they repeated the early morning activities, and they enjoyed it equally. After the love making, they both fell sound asleep, needing the rest before their long and tiring trip to Dallas.

At dawn they left for the trip back to Dallas. Having had no breakfast, they stopped at a diner in Selma and had coffee and flapjacks, then hurried to get back on the trail for home.

On the way Conchita asked, "Where are you going to live in Dallas?"

"I hadn't thought much about it; how about you?" Shawn answered.

"Well, I guess I will have to move back in with my drunken daddy, no matter how much I hate to do it," she replied.

"Well, maybe not. I would really like for us to live together, but Mama would have an Irish hissy fit if we did that before we are married," Shawn said.

"Not to mention what Father Lynch would think," she added.

"I'll tell you what. You find yourself a nice house, move my stuff into it, and then I will come and visit you whenever I can," Shawn offered.

"I can't afford that," she responded.

"No, but I can. I'll give you the money, and then we'll have a place to go when we are married," he explained.

"Oh, Shawn, are you proposing to me?" she excitedly asked.

"Yeah, I guess I am," he responded.

"Shawn, you sweetheart. You will never be sorry. I will be a good wife to you and be happy to have your children," she told him, then kissed him long and hard.

It was almost dark when Shawn took Conchita to her house and went in with her. Her dad would be no trouble to her tonight; he was passed out at the table, his head propped up on one of his arms and his hand still holding an empty liquor bottle.

They went back outside and Shawn gave her some money

to find a place, and Conchita promised to look for a nice place to live.

Shawn went directly to the boarding house, tended to the team, then went to the apartment, where he was met by Patrick and Patricia. Shawn had to tell them all about his trip. Then he explained that he and Conchita planned on being married and that she was going to look for a place to live until they were married; then he would move in with her.

They both congratulated him. Later Patrick got him alone and asked him, "Well, did you find out?"

"I sure as hell did, and that Indian girl lied to me," Shawn said smiling broadly.

"That's good. Now you know. We'll talk more about it later."

Shawn reported to the Ranger station the following morning and Darling introduced him to the other Rangers he would be working with. He recognized four of them from the showdown at the Dallas Palace: Paul Hagan, Bill Falco, George Lynch, and Swede Jorgenson. He also met six other Rangers and would meet the others when they returned from their assignments. Darling partnered Shawn with Swede Jorgenson. Swede was a tall, raw-boned man with broad shoulders and chiseled facial features. He constantly had his lower lip lined with snuff. Then Swede showed Shawn around the station, and then the two of them went to lunch at a diner close to the station.

Then the two of them were assigned to patrol the east side of Garland. Normally this area would be handled by the sheriff's department, but today they had been left short-handed by an outbreak of food poisoning, so the sheriff asked Captain Darling for help.

Their only excitement for that afternoon was to break up a fist fight in front of a saloon frequented by oil well workers. One of the Swede's gun butts to the head of the most belligerent combatant ended the fight, and they both continued their patrol.

They finished out their week with other routine assignments.

Sunday morning the whole family went to mass together then adjourned to their mother's house for dinner. As was customary on Sunday, J.B. arranged for two chefs from the Palace to come to the house and prepare dinner for all of them.

After a delicious dinner of roast beef, baked potatoes, and green beans, the men all adjourned to the porch to smoke. The women all huddled in the parlor to talk and welcome Conchita into their family. Pam suggested that she, Linda, and Conchita all have a triple wedding with the three brothers. Patricia and Anna agreed this would be a beautiful thing to happen to the Sweeney family. Anna promised to ask J.B. for his opinion and to ask Father Lynch if he could perform such a ceremony.

By the time of the following Sunday's dinner, J.B. thought it was a good idea, Father Lynch indicated it could be done, and it seemed everyone knew about it except Shawn, Joseph, and Mark. Pam and Linda had gotten approval of their parents, Conchita needed no approval from her drunken daddy, and Patrick and Patricia thought it would be a terrific idea.

CHAPTER 23

# A TRIPLE WEDDING FOR THE SWEENEY BROTHERS

When the boys were approached about the wedding plans, they were not surprised. Their mother had been making decisions for them all of their lives and apparently had no idea of stopping now.

The only thing to be decided now was the date. Shawn would have to check with Captain Darling when he could have some time off. It all depended on the answer he got as to when the final plans could be made. When Shawn reported for work the next morning he received another surprise. The hijacking of crude oil shipments from Dallas to the refinery at Nacogdoches had become so commonplace that the governor requested the Rangers accompany each shipment until the bandits were caught and punished. It was expected to take at least a month, so Shawn did not even bother to mention to Darling his upcoming marriage plans.

When Shawn told the family that evening, everyone was disappointed but understood he had chosen this career, and they would all just have to wait until this job was finished. Most of the robberies were happening on the highway about halfway between Dallas and Nacogdoches.

Darling's plan was to station six Rangers in the small town of Linn, where they could respond when an attack happened. Twelve other Rangers would be assigned to travel with the oil shipments, two Rangers to each shipment.

Shawn and his partner Swede would be with those assigned to Linn. There were no available living quarters available for them in Linn, so they pitched two large tents. One tent would house the Rangers, and the other their horses.

It was a boring job, so some days the Rangers would ride several miles up and down Nacogdoches highway, waiting for the tanker wagons and hoping to intercept the bandits.

They had been there six days and watched at least a dozen tanker wagons pass without incident.

One morning riding north, they heard gunfire ahead. Galloping to the scene, they met the wagon, driven by two bandits, instead of the teamsters, who would later be found dead along the road.

When they approached the wagon, they identified themselves as Texas Rangers and ordered the bandits to surrender. Their request was met with gunfire. Swede and Shawn returned gunfire, killed the driver, and wounded his accomplice. Shawn had also been hit in the shoulder and knocked from his horse. Swede then killed the wounded bandit with a shot between the eyes, then rushed to assist Shawn.

It was obvious to Swede that Shawn was badly injured. He was bleeding profusely, and had no use of his left arm. Swede bandaged the wound as best he could, put Shawn on the horse with him, and rode as fast as he could toward someplace where he could get the help of a doctor. His horse was on the verge of collapse from carrying double at a fast gallop. When he came to a wide place in the road, with no name, but with a saloon and general store, he carried Shawn into the general store and was met by the owners. Adolph and Hilda Schmidt were a middle-aged German couple who sold groceries, grain, supplies, and also ran the post office and telegraph office. Hilda wasted no time in putting Shawn on a table and changed the bandages on his shoulder. Swede asked Adolph to send the following wire for him. It read:

> *To Captain Darling, Texas Ranger Station, Garland, Texas:*
>
> *Urgent. Sweeney and me intercepted two oil hijackers and killed them both. Sweeney seriously wounded in shoulder. Brought him to general store on Nacogdoches highway about ten miles north of Linn.*
>
> *Need immediate medical attention for Sweeney.*
>
> *Signed,*<br>*Ranger Jorgenson*

It was less than half an hour when the following wire came in:

> To Ranger Jorgenson:
> Good work. Have dispatched ambulance wagon and doctor. Should be there in three hours. Take care of Sweeney.
>
> Captain Darling

After he read the wire he went to check on Shawn. He was awake, but in a lot of pain. Hilda had managed to slow down the bleeding, but his left arm remained useless. Adolph then came to them with a bottle of brandy, saying, "Here, give him a shot of this. It might ease his pain a little."

Swede replied, "Thank you sir, and I think I'll have a little myself."

Swede told Shawn to drink as much as he could, and in a few minutes it helped ease his pain. Then Swede turned up the bottle and took a good drink himself. It was slightly more than two hours when the ambulance arrived. It was pulled by a team of six white horses. A doctor rushed into the general store and went directly to Shawn.

After a brief examination he announced, "My name is Dr. Diego. I'm afraid this man has had a bullet break his collarbone. Apparently the bullet went on through but left a nasty exit wound. I think we had better get him to Garland General Hospital as soon as the horses are rested a little. He has lost a lot of blood."

Swede then told Shawn, "I have three dead men back down the road a spell and a load of oil to tend to, but as soon as

I get that done, I'll ride to Garland and check on you at the hospital."

Swede thanked the Schmidts, told Dr. Diego he would see him later at the hospital, then rode back to Linn to get some other Rangers to help him load the three dead bodies and take the shipment of oil to the refinery. That completed, he rode off to Garland to check on Shawn.

When he arrived at the hospital he found the entire Sweeney family huddled in the visitors' lounge. Conchita was also there crying and saying, "I told Shawn he was doing a dangerous job."

Anna was trying to console her, but also had tears in her eyes. Pam and Linda were also present. Swede took time to tell them all exactly what happened, when Anna told him, "Thank you, Swede, for looking after my boy."

It was about fifteen minutes later when Dr. Diego came into the lounge telling them, "Mrs. Rich, your son is going to be alright. We got the wound cleaned up, and the bleeding stopped. We tried to bandage it so the shoulder blade would grow back together, but I'm not sure that will work. Only time will tell. We're going to have to keep him here for five or six days to make sure there is no infection, and to feed him with a diet that will let his body make a lot of blood to replace part of the blood he lost. After that, you can take him home, but he will need someone to give him constant care."

Conchita spoke up, "I can do that, doctor. I just rented a house, and I will stay with him 24 hours a day."

"And who might you be?" Dr. Diego asked.

"I am Conchita, and I am his fiancé," Conchita responded.

"Well, if that's OK with his family, it's OK with me," Dr. Diego remarked.

Anna agreed, and so it was settled. Then they were permitted to go in and visit Shawn, but only two at a time. Conchita waited until the rest of the family visited with Shawn, then went in last to tell him about the house she had rented and how she was going to look after him when the hospital released him.

She stayed so long, the nurse finally had to run her out so Shawn could get some sleep.

Patrick and Patricia had remained behind to take her home. She showed them the cute little bungalow she had rented, and when they entered they saw Shawn's items they had purchased for him.

Patricia told her, "This is just beautiful. I know Shawn will be comfortable here."

Patrick added, "I know you and Shawn will be comfortable here. I like it."

When Patrick and Patricia were riding home Patricia asked, "I wonder what Father Lynch will think about the two of them living here together before they are married?"

"I don't think he will object, under the circumstances. He is a practical man," Patrick answered.

Conchita went to see Shawn every day and even asked the nurse to show her how to change the bandages for after she had him at home.

Many days Anna or Patricia came with her, but they were not as regular a visitor as was Conchita.

On the sixth day J.B. hired an ambulance, and they transported Shawn to his new home. He was delighted to see the home and how Conchita had decorated it. The two attendants carried Shawn to the bed Conchita had prepared for him.

Father Lynch came by to visit Shawn that afternoon and stayed for coffee. He not only approved the arrangement, but he blessed the house before he left.

Then he told Shawn, "I will pray for your speedy recovery. Not only am I anxious for you to heal properly, but I am anxious to perform the first triple wedding I have ever done."

That said, Father Lynch rode off.

Shawn's recovery went well. Conchita became very proficient changing his bandages every day and looking for an infection, but there was none. Anna came to see him every day, and J.B. came with her at least once a week. His brothers were also weekly visitors as was Father Lynch, Captain Darling, and Dr. Diego.

With the wound healing nicely, the only worry now was the healing of the collarbone. Three weeks passed, and Shawn could move his arm, but still did not have full use of it.

He could now sit up in a chair for his meals, and he was able to walk short distances, but he still had to keep his arm in a sling.

By the fifth week Shawn called the family together and announced he was feeling well enough to set a date for the wedding.

The Macauley sisters giggled and everyone had their spirits raised by this news. It was decided to have the wedding two Saturdays from this date. That would give them time to invite family and friends and alert Father Lynch. Conchita produced a bottle of bourbon and everyone drank a toast to the three brides-to-be.

That evening Conchita fixed them potato soup and cornbread, then told Shawn, "Now, you get back in bed. You've had enough excitement for today."

"I will if you will go to bed with me. I think I can stand some more excitement this evening," Shawn said.

"OK, you naughty boy. I thought you would never ask. Just you be careful and don't get that wound bleeding again. You just lie still, and I'll do all the work," Conchita told him.

Conchita was very careful as she slithered on top of him from the right side being very careful to avoid his left arm and shoulder. Shawn used his good right arm to move from massaging first her left breast, then her right one, and soon they were in a rhythm that resulted in ecstasy for both of them.

Then they stayed very still for a long time, holding each other, kissing, and telling each other how much they loved each other. Then Conchita carefully got off of him, laid beside him, and they both were soon sleeping sounder than either of them had in a long time.

They both slept later than usual, but Conchita was up first making coffee for them.

Shawn gave Conchita money, and while Anna stayed with him, Patricia accompanied Conchita to purchase a wedding dress. The two weeks were passing quickly with so much to do.

Patricia wrote her father, and he replied he would be there. He had to miss her wedding but he would sure make this one. Conchita went by to see her daddy, but his reply was, "Hell, no. I won't go. I don't want anything to do with those rich people, and you'll be sorry if you do."

Of course Pam and Linda invited their parents and knew

they would attend. Shawn invited Captain Darling and Swede, and they both agreed to attend. He also invited Major Evans and Lefty, and got only a tentative yes, subject to duties.

Patrick and J.B. invited Jim Stock and George Lumley, the other directors of the Dallas Palace. Anna invited all of her church friends. Patricia also invited Mary and Mabel, her employees from the boarding house. Joseph invited Charles Goodnight, who said he would attend.

It was agreed William Macauley would escort both of his daughters down the aisle, and J.B. would escort Conchita.

Pam and Linda had friends who would serve as bridesmaids for them. Patricia would be matron of honor for Conchita. Mark, Joseph, Shawn, and Patrick all wanted to wear the Sweeney blazers they had worn to Anna and J.B.'s wedding.

The large church was packed to overflowing. Father Lynch remarked the church was the most crowded he had seen it since midnight mass last Christmas. It was filled with a diverse group of people from several walks of life. Colonel Mallory stood out in his full dress blue uniform.

The four Rangers drew attention in their Ranger working uniforms of starched blue jeans and white western shirts with the familiar star in a wheel badge proudly displayed on the front

J.B. Rich showed up in a tuxedo, as did Jim Stock and George Lumley. Father Lynch said a short mass, and then had each couple, in turn, recite their vows. Then after a kiss, they were husbands and wives.

The newlyweds escaped the church, jumped into waiting buggies, and were whisked off to the Dallas Palace. The Palace was decorated even more finely than it had been for J.B. and

Anna's wedding. Three large tables were loaded with every kind of food imaginable.

There was a bar set up with three bartenders. Charles Goodnight, now in his 80s, showed up with a young girl he introduced as Miss Goodnight. He later told J.B. and Anna in confidence he had started writing to her, attracted to her because she was the only person he knew named Goodnight. He even confided he intended to marry her.

All three brides looked so beautiful in their bridal gowns, it would have been impossible to tell which was the prettiest. Shawn stood out from his three brothers. Even though they all looked nice in their blue blazers, Shawn was the only one with his left arm in a sling.

Even though there was a lot of eating snacks and drinking champagne and hard liquor, there were no problems. After an hour, everyone sat down to a lavish dinner of roast beef, baked potatoes, grits, green salad, and biscuits or cornbread. J.B. rose and proposed a toast to the three newly married couples. Everyone drank to them, and then gave them a standing ovation.

After everyone had eaten their fill, the chefs brought in a very large, three-tiered wedding cake. The three brides cut the cake and passed out slices to their husbands and guests at the main table. Then waiters came and cut more cake and served the people at the three other tables.

Then more champagne was served to all of the guests.

While the revelry continued, it was easy for the three couples to slip out and drive away in their new surreys that J.B. and Anna had given them for wedding presents.

At the head table Anna noticed tears in Dorothy Macauley's

eyes when she realized Pam and Linda were gone. Anna attempted to console her, but also had tears in her eyes. J.B. and William Macauley tried to console both of them.

So this is Anna's story of her five sons. The hardships she had faced were many, especially with the death of her first husband and second son, Samuel. However, all of her heartaches were forgotten as she witnessed her remaining sons happily married this day. It was the end of an era, but the beginning of another.